THE FAMILIARS
PALACE of DREAMS

Adam Jay Epstein
Andrew Jacobson

Art by Dave Phillips

The Familiars #4: Palace of Dreams
Text copyright © 2014 by Adam Jay Epstein and Andrew Jacobson
Illustrations copyright © 2014 by Dave Phillips

ISBN 978-0-06-212029-8

Typography by Erin Fitzsimmons
13 14 15 16 17 CG/RRDH 10 9 8 7 6 5 4 3 2 1
❖
First Edition

For my mom, who always believes in me.
—A. J. E.

For Willa, my daughter.
Never stop following your dreams.
—A. J.

CONTENTS

1

QUESTABOUT

According to Vastian folklore, the island was haunted, and one look at the solitary castle clinging to the isle's bloodred cliffs left little doubt in Aldwyn's mind that the ghost stories were true.

"Yeardley, here we come," Jack said.

Aldwyn's heart skipped a beat, excited by the thought of reuniting with the twin sister he had been separated from since birth.

Aldwyn and Jack's two-man sailing skiff rapidly approached the treacherous shallows. Despite the danger, it was the only route to shore. Looking at his familiar, the young wizard in training added, "Won't be long now!"

The Maidenmere cat stood at the bow, his claws digging into the waterlogged wooden planks. His loyal was scrambling in back, tightening the lines for their arrival.

"Prepare the anchor for landing," Jack called out.

"Aye, aye, Captain," Aldwyn replied, giving the boy a salute with his paw.

Aldwyn flipped the deck chest open, pulled out the anchor, and uncoiled its rope. But not with his paws. He did it with his mind. Like all the cats of Maidenmere, Aldwyn possessed the magical talent of telekinesis, and he was getting better at it all the time.

He looked back up from the rocky crags to the castle. If his last few months of investigation proved correct, Yeardley would be inside. Word had it that she'd been sold to a justiciary from the Equitas Isles, and by all accounts this cursed island in the Beyond, over one hundred miles south of the Vastian border, was where the high judge could be found holding her as his pet, or perhaps against her will as a captive.

"Aldwyn, hold on!" Jack shouted, pointing to a

bubbling in the water ahead.

Suddenly the ocean erupted. A giant sea scorpion burst forth, the razor-sharp stinger at the end of its tail whipping from side to side. Their only options were to either retreat or meet the scorpion head-on.

Aldwyn and Jack's vessel barreled straight for it.

Jack was already chanting: "Rooster's feather, buttered crumpet, ocean winds, sound the trumpet!"

A wave crashed against the bow and its spray formed into the shape of a horn. Then a gust of wind blew through it, sending out a bellowing call. The sound didn't stop the beast looming before them. If anything, the scorpion was angered even more, its pincers snapping menacingly. But the magical trumpet wasn't created to cause fear. It was to call for help.

The sailing skiff began to rise up from the water. There beneath them they saw a traveling whale, lifting the boat high above the surf. The scorpion didn't have time to react before the great blueback's forehead rammed into the creature, cracking open its exoskeleton like an eggshell.

The whale continued to charge forward, crushing the scorpion's shattered remains against the rocky crag.

"We owe you one!" Jack called out to the whale, who continued to carry the skiff on its back.

"I know they say it's nice to have friends in high places, but it doesn't hurt to have a few underwater, either," Aldwyn said.

As the inlet became shallower, the blueback was forced to slow, dipping its head and allowing the sailing skiff to slip gently into the waters. Aldwyn and Jack coasted for the gravel beach, while the whale turned for the sea, giving a farewell blast of spray from its six blowholes.

The front of the skiff ran ashore, its wooden hull clattering against the bed of pebbles beneath.

"Anchors away," Jack instructed Aldwyn.

Aldwyn telekinetically flung the iron wedge far enough up the beach so that its metal points embedded themselves deep in the sand. The rope went taut, preventing the sailing vessel from getting dragged back into the ocean.

Jack made sure the leather component pouch across his chest and the wand tucked into his belt were secure. Then he pulled a short sword from his sheath and clambered out of the boat. Aldwyn, armed with nothing more than his mind, followed him across the bleak landscape. Pebble crabs and land lobsters scurried out of their way as they walked toward the zigzagging staircase carved into the cliff's side, which was splintered with cracks.

Since their first conversation in Kalstaff's cottage at Stone Runlet, loyal and familiar had dreamed of being Beyonders, going on adventures like this together. They hadn't been sent out on a mission—just the two of them alone—until now. And so far, their quest had exceeded Aldwyn's highest hopes.

"It's been said that for many who climb to the top of those stairs, it's a one-way trip." The words came out of Jack's mouth in a whisper.

"If you're trying to scare me, you're going to have to do better than that," Aldwyn said.

"It's not rust or sandstone that give those cliffs their crimson color. It's blood."

"Okay, that was better," Aldwyn said with a shudder.

They began to climb, taking one narrow step at a time. Inside the castle at the top of the cliff, people came from far and wide to stand before the justiciary. They came with arguments, disputes, and moral quandaries that no house of trials, royal court, or council elder could solve. If a decision was made in their favor, they descended the staircase happy. If not, they took a faster way down. The specters of those fallen bodies were said to haunt the cliffs.

"Go to your happy place, go to your happy place," Aldwyn said. "An all-you-can-eat fish buffet."

"I think you've been spending a little too much time with Gilbert," Jack replied.

It was true. Aldwyn's easily panicked tree frog best friend had been rubbing off on him. But even the rarely rattled Skylar, the third member of the Prophesized Three, would have been unnerved by the otherworldly screams that whistled through the rocks.

Of course, Gilbert and Skylar were on their own questabouts with their loyals, far from this haunted isle.

After the dust had settled from the defeat of

Paksahara—Queen Loranella's traitorous hare familiar—life in Vastia returned to normal, with human and animal ruling the queendom together. In the months following the destruction of the Dead Army of zombie animals Paksahara raised from the ground, Aldwyn, Skylar, and Gilbert resumed their training with their wizard companions inside the protective walls of Bronzhaven. Side by side, familiar and loyal worked to strengthen their magical bond.

Now they had all been sent on separate missions—wizarding rites of passage—to test what they had learned. Gilbert and Marianne had traveled to the Ocean Oracle to seek the ancient *Protocols of Divination*, a rare tome offering insight into the art of clairvoyance. Skylar and Dalton were off searching for the lost Xylem garden of the great forest communer, Horteus Ebekenezer. And Aldwyn and Jack were here, perhaps on the most dangerous quest of all. To find Aldwyn's sister.

"What do I say when I see her?" Aldwyn asked.

"Didn't you tell me your sister reads minds?"

Jack replied. "Maybe you won't need to say anything at all."

"I'm serious, Jack. The only other family member I've ever met tried to kill me. Multiple times. I just want this to go well."

Aldwyn was starting to feel dizzy and off balance, and not just because the steps below his paws were nearly crumbling. It was that he had built up so much hope for this moment. Now he was merely a few flights away.

"Why don't you start with, 'Hey, I'm your long-lost twin brother, Aldwyn,'" Jack suggested. "She cries. You hug. Big happy family reunion. Then we ask nicely if she can leave with us."

"And if the justiciary refuses?" Aldwyn asked. "We don't know if he's a friend or foe."

"Well, that's why I brought this," Jack said, gesturing with his short sword.

"What's it like having a sister, anyway?"

"Pretty annoying actually. If she's anything like my sister, Marianne, you've come a long way to find someone who'll tease and humiliate you for the rest of your life."

The two shared a smile.

Just then, Aldwyn felt a viselike grip tighten around his tail. Long, slender fingers with pointy nails reached out from the underside of the staircase. Aldwyn pulled free, losing a tuft of fur in the process. More arms were emerging from the rocks, and the specters of the isle began slipping out from the cracks in the cliff's side. Their faces were narrow, their mouths twisted in a permanent scream.

Jack swung his sword at one of the attacking specters. The blade cut directly through the ghostly figure and struck the wall behind it.

Aldwyn lifted a chunk of crumbling step with his mind and hurled it at another of the vengeful spirits. Once again the attempt was in vain.

"Owww!" Jack cried.

One of the specters' nails had dug into his arm, leaving a trail of blood from his elbow down to his wrist. It seemed that while these haunted beings could not be harmed by blade or stone, they could easily hurt the living.

Very quickly Aldwyn and Jack's path up the staircase was blocked by a swarm of moaning specters.

"What do we do now?" Aldwyn asked.

"We find another way to the castle," Jack said, whipping out his wand and pointing it skyward. "Hop on."

Aldwyn grabbed hold of his loyal's leg, and the two, led by Jack's wand, took flight. But they didn't get far before one of the specters ripped the wand from Jack's hand, sending them into a free fall.

As they tumbled through the air, Jack stabbed his sword at the cliff's side. The blade scraped along the rocks, leaving a trail of sparks in its wake. The specters shrieked and howled, frightened by the flecks of electricity. The tip of Jack's sword wedged itself into a thin crevice, stopping their fall. But Aldwyn could see the stone was splintering around the sword, and the wicked ghosts—no longer deterred by the sparks—were back in pursuit.

Aldwyn flipped open Jack's component pouch and telekinetically tossed a dozen storm berries at the specters. Tiny gray clouds appeared, accompanied by rain and lightning. The sparking bolts sent the ghosts back into a panic, forcing them to retreat into the cracks in the cliff.

"Good thing Skylar made us take those berries," Jack said.

"She always says nothing helps out in a pinch like storm berries," Aldwyn replied. "And to never leave home without them."

"Now how do we get out of here?" Jack asked, feet dangling in midair.

Aldwyn glanced around. They were too far from the staircase to grab hold of it. The sword was giving way. And those storm clouds weren't going to last forever.

"We're slipping," Jack said as the stone around the metal tip began to crumble.

Then the blade dislodged itself from the mountainside and Jack and Aldwyn dropped like two stones. Speeding toward the ground, Aldwyn scanned the beach for something that might save them. Anything. Then he spied a polished wooden rod amid the pebbles: Jack's wand! He focused all his attention and snatched it up with his mind. Just before they made impact, the wand flew into Jack's hand. They immediately changed course, soaring to the top of the cliffs, never slowing until they touched down outside the castle keep.

"We were nearly food for the worms," Jack said.

"An all-too-common feeling in my life," Aldwyn replied.

"But better than actually being food for the worms," Jack said.

"I can't argue with that."

Unlike the collapsing staircase that led up to it, the justiciary's castle was an imposing fortress of solid steel. It stood three stories tall, with pikes lining the perimeter of the rooftop. Scales of justice were engraved on the front doors. One side weighed a severed hand choking a snake; the other the silhouette of a dove rising up from a flaming nest. The walls popped and sizzled, emitting some kind of electrical energy. Even from a distance, it made the fur on Aldwyn's back stand on end.

Jack headed for the door, but Aldwyn hesitated. It was as if his paws were trapped in quickmud. He was so close yet he hardly felt ready.

"Come on, Aldwyn," Jack said. "Meeting your sister is the one thing on this island that you shouldn't be afraid of."

Aldwyn pictured seeing Yeardley for the first time since he was a day-old kitten and took a calming breath. He joined Jack at the castle's entrance. Jack reached out his fist and rapped his knuckles on the door. The two waited. For a moment it seemed like no one was going to answer. Then the door was pulled inward by a large, bearded man dressed in scuffed leather armor. He was holding a metal staff that crackled at the tip. Bright white sparks filled the air. Upon seeing Jack and Aldwyn, he lowered it, extinguishing the sparks.

"You never know when one of those specters will try and sneak its way inside," he said. "I wish you'd sent a messenger arrow to alert me to your arrival. I would have met you down at the beach. It's a miracle you made it up here alive without one of these."

The guard gave his sparking staff a little pat.

"We're here to see the justiciary," Jack said.

"I could have guessed as much," the man joked. "We don't get too many tourists coming around here."

He opened the door wider and allowed them entrance.

Aldwyn and Jack followed the guard down a long hallway to a spacious room with a wooden chair and table sitting atop a dais. Dozens of troubled Vastians lined the hall, many embroiled in heated arguments. It was clear they had come to state their cases before the justiciary.

"Do you have any idea how long we'll need to wait?" Jack asked.

"Well, that depends on when he returns," the guard replied.

"Returns?" Jack asked.

"Yes. The justiciary's services were requested by the Legion of Mindcasters. He's been absent for some time now."

"Ask him about Yeardley," Aldwyn urged Jack.

"What about the Maidenmere cat he keeps by his side? Is she here?"

"Oh, no. The justiciary never travels without her. That black-and-white is a very powerful ally."

"And this Legion of Mindcasters," Jack said. "Do you know where they are located?"

"I'm afraid that's confidential, young man. Top secret."

But the answer wasn't good enough for Aldwyn.

15

His eyes narrowed in on the guard. He focused his mental energy the same way he did for telekinesis, only this time he wasn't trying to move anything. He was attempting to read the man's mind.

Aldwyn had only recently discovered that he had inherited his mother's telepathic powers. They were still developing, and he had yet to learn how to control them. Months of practice had not helped, as his readings were spotty at best. Still, he concentrated, trying to open the guard's brain like a book.

Suddenly words came into his head: *Well of Ashtheril.*

Aldwyn knew that's where Yeardley and the justiciary were.

"Aldwyn, what is it?" Jack asked, sensing something.

"We can go now," Aldwyn said.

Jack nodded and the two turned for the door.

You shouldn't have done that, cat. You shouldn't have pried.

Aldwyn looked back, but it was clear he hadn't heard the words spoken aloud. It was what the guard was thinking. And now he was aiming the reignited sparking tip of his metal staff at them.

"Usually, I only use this on those vile cliff ghosts," the guard said. "But today I'm going to make an exception."

He fired off a blast of lightning that shot right between Aldwyn and Jack.

"*Trussilium bindus!*" Jack shouted.

A silver rope materialized in his hand and he threw the coiled end around the staff. With a tug it flew into Jack's waiting palm. Aldwyn used his telekinesis to push open the front doors, and as he leaped onto the back of Jack's tunic, the two made a running jump off the edge of the cliff.

Jack's wand guided them through the air as the crackling staff kept the specters at bay.

"So, where to next?" Jack asked.

"The Well of Ashtheril," Aldwyn called back.

"The what? I've never heard of it."

"Neither have I. But wherever it is, we'll find it. We have to."

Jack pointed the wand down toward the beached ship. Aldwyn was disappointed that they'd be leaving the Equitas Isles without Yeardley. But their trip had provided him with an important clue. He was another step closer to his sister. And he knew that with the help of his companions back in Bronzhaven, he would find her.

2

A BIRTHDAY SURPRISE

"Tighter . . . tighter. Too tight."

Gilbert was wrapped head to toe in seaweed and looked like a slimy green mummy. A young palace hand stood in the spa waters loosening the kelp around the tree frog's ankle.

"All that's missing is a pair of chopsticks and some soy sauce," Aldwyn said from the gilded archway at the entrance to the Bronzhaven seaweed springs.

Gilbert leaped to his feet, nearly falling face-first into the water.

"Aldwyn, you're back!" He removed the mask covering his eyes and ran over to his friend. "So, did you find her?"

"Not yet," Aldwyn replied. "And I'm fairly certain the justiciary doesn't want her to be found. What about you? How was your questabout?"

"Surprisingly easy. When Marianne and I reached the Ocean Oracle, the Seven Serpent Guardians were absent. We just waltzed right in and asked for the tome." Gilbert peeled off the sheets of seaweed clinging to his body. "Just keep that between us, though. I might have told Skylar a slightly different story. One involving me beheading those Seven Guardians."

"You could have been honest with her, you know."

"Once you get immortalized in stained glass as a hero of the land, you don't want people to think you've gone soft."

"Are you ready for your flower petal massage, Master Gilbert?" asked the palace hand.

Gilbert's cheeks flushed pink with embarrassment, even through the green.

"We should go find Skylar," Gilbert said to

Aldwyn, quickly changing the subject. "I'm sure she'll be excited to see you."

Aldwyn nodded. It had been ten days since they'd all departed on their questabouts. He was happy to be back with his best friends, too. Especially since Commander Warden had sent Jack to meet up with Marianne and Dalton at Turnbuckle Academy. The most renowned beast tamers from the Beyond were gathered there for a series of lectures on monster baiting and entanglement techniques, rare and valuable wizarding skills.

Aldwyn and Gilbert walked beneath the archway, leaving the seaweed springs behind. They made their way through the palace courtyard, past the golden eel pond and the wishing web in the everwillow tree. Outside, preparations for a feast were under way, as kitchen wizards used their magic to summon fruit trees from the ground, complete with apples and pears ripe for the picking.

"Is this all for Queen Loranella's birthday?" Aldwyn asked.

"Yep," Gilbert replied. "The Council has

decided to throw her a surprise party. She and Galatea left early this morning to oversee the resummoning of Vastia's southern enchanted fences." Gilbert's voice lowered into a conspiratorial whisper. "Of course, that was just an excuse to get her out of the castle."

"It's too bad our loyals are going to miss this," Aldwyn said.

"Well, it's not every day you get to learn how to trap a sandtaur," Gilbert replied. "Of course, I'd rather be indulging in all-you-can-eat fun any day. Guess that's one of the perks of being in the Prophesized Three. You're a guest of honor at every royal function. Even other people's birthday parties!"

"That reminds me," Aldwyn said. "I don't have a present."

"Don't worry. Skylar took care of it. She got something special from all three of us."

They walked through an open doorway into a long corridor, where banners from every province hung on the walls. Guards and palace bulldogs roamed the grounds on routine watch.

"This way," Gilbert said, following a trail of

water trickling down a stairway. "Skylar collected some moist moss on her questabout. She's been experimenting with all sorts of liquefying spells ever since."

As Aldwyn and Gilbert climbed the steps, the water flow got heavier and they could hear the sound of splashing behind a closed wooden door.

"Now try the table," Sorceress Edna's high-pitched, nasal voice could be heard calling.

Aldwyn telekinetically turned the knob on the door, just in time to see a stone table transform into a gelatinous shell of itself before splashing down into a puddle. Skylar stood on the opposite side of the room, observing her handiwork.

"If you reverse the spell, you should be able to return the table back into its original shape," Sorceress Edna said between sips from a cup of blueberry tea.

Skylar plucked another talonful of moss from her satchel and squeezed it as she incanted: *"Suti-tauqa, sutitauqa!"*

The blue jay's wings trembled, and the silver-and-emerald chain of the Noctonati she wore around her ankle rattled. Suddenly the water began to transform. But not back into a table. Just a pool of stone.

"That's going to take a little more practice," Skylar said.

"Look who I found," Gilbert said.

Skylar turned to see Aldwyn avoiding the wet spots on the floor. She flapped over and wrapped her wings around him in a hug.

"Welcome home," she said. "Did you find Yeardley?"

Aldwyn shook his head. "Have you ever heard of the Well of Ashtheril?"

"No. Why? Is that where she is?"

"I think so."

"We'll check the queen's library," Skylar said. "We were able to locate the Crown of the Snow Leopard. We should be able to find a simple well."

"I figured I could count on you," Aldwyn said, happy the Prophesized Three were together again.

"You know me. The older and dustier a book, the better." Skylar tipped her beak up into the air. "Why do I smell seaweed?"

"Oh, Gilbert was—"

Before Aldwyn could finish, Gilbert cut him off.

24

"—just wondering the same thing," the tree frog said. "Must be from those liquefying spells you were casting."

Skylar shrugged.

"I'll let the three of you catch up," Sorceress Edna said, waddling toward the door. "I need to get ready for tonight's party."

Skylar opened up her satchel and showed Aldwyn what was inside.

"You wouldn't believe all the neat stuff we took from the Xylem garden. Icari weed, marble bark, snizzle grass. And a dozen other things we haven't even been able to identify yet."

Gilbert walked over munching on an orange root.

"This carrot tastes funny," he said.

"Gilbert, that's not a carrot," Skylar said.

"Then what is it?" asked the tree frog.

"We don't know. It's one of the twelve things we haven't identified! But it most likely has some very powerful magic associated with it."

Gilbert gave a panicked look and tried to cough up whatever he was eating, but nothing came out. They all waited in anticipation.

"I don't feel anything," Gilbert said.

"Well, if your body begins to expand rapidly, stay away from any sharp objects," Skylar replied.

Quick footsteps could be heard coming up the stairs. Commander Warden entered the room, his black hair swept back into a ponytail. Dressed in gold studded armor and leather pants, he had the look of a man who could lead a thousand soldiers into battle. The commander dropped to one knee, bringing himself down to Aldwyn, Skylar, and Gilbert's eye level.

"In case you thought you'd be getting a vacation while your loyals are at Turnbuckle, I'm afraid you won't be so lucky. I have a full schedule planned for you. We start first thing in the morning."

"Whoa," Gilbert said. "Aldwyn just got home. He's probably exhausted. Give this cat a break. Let him kick up his paws."

"I'm fine, Gilbert," Aldwyn said.

"You don't have to impress anyone," Gilbert said. "It's okay to want a little downtime. Some relaxation. At least wait until tomorrow afternoon. No one would blame you."

"You can reschedule your mud bath, Gilbert,"

Commander Warden said.

Gilbert was about to protest, but thought better of it.

"Yes, sir."

"Good. The three of you will find that I'm not nearly as lenient as Kalstaff was when he taught you. And Sorceress Edna may be prickly, but you won't find me sipping blueberry tea during my lessons. Queen Loranella put me in charge of your next stage of training for a reason. When I was headmaster at Turnbuckle Academy, I could squeeze magic out of even the most common squire. With pupils who have potential for greatness within them, such as you three, I will bring out magnificence. We'll meet at the archery range at sunrise."

"You know I can't fire a bow, right?" Skylar asked, gesturing to her wings.

"You won't need bows. I have something else in store for you." Commander Warden flashed them a smile. "I'll see you at the party this evening. I know the queen will appreciate you all being there."

Just then Gilbert let out a sudden belch, and a

burst of fire shot from his mouth. It nearly singed the feathers off Skylar's body.

"Cinder beet, of course," Skylar said, pointing a wing at the half-eaten orange stick. "Thanks, Gilbert. Now I've only got eleven things left to identify."

Gilbert was already lapping up water from one of the puddles on the ground. Steam poured from his nostrils.

"If you're still hungry, I'm really curious what this black mushroom does." Skylar pulled another mystery component from her pouch.

A loud roar split the air, silencing the party guests gathered in the courtyard. Aldwyn looked up, past the colorful streamers and paper lanterns magically floating in the night sky, to see a chinchilla sitting on the palace wall, pointing its tiny paw into the distance.

"The queens have arrived at the gates of Bronzhaven!" the palace crier announced.

The friends and colleagues of Loranella all twittered excitedly as they took their positions, hoping to surprise the queen. Aldwyn had strategically placed himself directly beside the appetizer table, where platters of raw fish were lined up. Sorceress Edna was pushing people into place, shuffling her short legs across the stone paths with her familiar, the minx Stolix, sitting on her shoulder.

"Quiet, everyone!" she shouted.

After the signal, Skylar flew overhead alongside four other birds from the Nearhurst Aviary. With a swoop and a spin, together they cast a grand illusion, making it appear as if all the guests were suddenly gone.

The thundering steps of Galatea, the lightmare queen, could be heard charging closer. Loranella sat atop her as they entered the courtyard and slowed to a stop. The queen dismounted.

"We made good progress today," Loranella said.

"Yes," Galatea replied. "But Vastia's reconstruction has only just begun. There will be much work to do."

"Then it is fortunate that we will be doing it together," Loranella said.

Aldwyn looked upon the human queen, her white shoulder-length hair wind-tossed from travel. She adjusted the seven-pronged golden crown atop her head. Her eyes glanced to the empty palace grounds, and although she seemed to be trying to hide it, Aldwyn saw what appeared to be a slight grin. He couldn't help but think that while it was well intentioned to throw the queen such an elaborately plotted party, attempting to surprise one as wise as Loranella was a hopeless endeavor indeed.

Skylar and her avian cohorts dropped the illusion, and as the hundreds gathered were revealed, they screamed out a collective "Surprise!"

Queen Loranella made a show of astonishment, and she smiled as the entire crowd broke out into song.

> Dragons rise and moons set on another merry
>   year!
> We wish you bowls of lifeseed and dreams that
>   have no fear!
> From every corner friends have come to join
>   and gather here!
> We celebrate this joyous day with giant shouts
>   of cheer!

And with that, they broke into reverential applause. Loranella quieted them.

"Thank you. I am truly humbled to see all of you tonight. It has been a year of great turmoil, the likes of which have not been seen since I was a young wizard. But we persevered. Our defeat of Paksahara and her Dead Army will live on in the history scrolls, long after I go to the Tomorrowlife. Until then, we'll keep the torches burning high and our glasses filled with persimmon wine."

Aldwyn spied a flute of purple bubbly and telekinetically lifted it from a table into Loranella's hand. As she held it up, the crowd shouted as one, "Vastia!"

Music began to play from an enchanted harp in the corner of the courtyard. It was Aldwyn's cue to make his move on the fish hors d'oeuvres, but just before he pounced, a hand touched his back.

"Aldwyn, I want you to meet somebody." It was Sorceress Edna, and she was pulling Aldwyn toward a man who appeared to have only half a face. One eye, one nostril, and a crooked half grin. It was as if someone started painting a picture and stopped in the middle. "This is Nazkareth, Loranella's second cousin."

"An honor, Prophesized One," said Nazkareth. "I have read of your travels. I'm most fascinated by your discovery of the mawpi's lair in the Beyond. At some point, I'd be very eager for you to lead me there."

"Yes, well, we'll have to see if that can be arranged," Aldwyn replied, still mesmerized by the man's deformity.

"Sooner rather than later," Nazkareth said, more insistently.

Before Aldwyn could respond to Nazkareth's demand, Sorceress Edna waved over a pair of dignitaries dressed in earth-toned garb.

"Aldwyn," she interrupted, "these are the twin druids of the Ratskeever province. They wanted to invite you to be an honored guest at their Festival of Alchemy."

"We wish to welcome the saviors of Vastia to our province." The more delicate of the two gave a graceful bow.

"You haven't truly dined until you've tasted the sweet nectar of a Ratskeever fig," her twin added.

"We're quite busy with our training right now," Aldwyn said, "but should we travel east of the Yennep, we'll be sure to pay you a visit."

In the months following the Prophesized Three's victory over Paksahara, Aldwyn had been introduced to hundreds of strangers. While it seemed that every one of them knew who he was, to him their names and faces were a blur. Even ones as memorable as Nazkareth and the twin druids of Ratskeever faded in time.

"If you'll excuse me," Aldwyn said, spying Navid and Marati, a king cobra and white-tailed mongoose, across the courtyard.

As he walked away, Aldwyn could hear Sorceress Edna speaking to the twin druids.

"Those are two of the seven animals that formed the circle of heroes," she said. "They've become officers in the Vastian guard, leading an elite squadron of animals and humans known as the Nightfall Battalion. Their mission is to root out any last traitors hiding across the fair queendom."

Edna's voice faded as Aldwyn approached the duo.

"Aldwyn, good, you can settle a debate for us," Marati said. "We recently encountered a tunneler dragon ransacking the northern mountain town of Glatar. Who would you say deserves credit for the kill? The soldier who crippled the beast and battered it to its wheezing end? Or the one who merely robbed it of its last breath?"

"Mind you, the dragon was still looking for innocents to spear when my venom blast struck its skull," Navid hissed back.

The two had once been mortal enemies, but now were the strongest of friends. Of course, there was still a healthy dose of competition between them.

"It could hardly bear its own weight by then," Marati replied.

"Tell that to the woman and child who nearly got skewered!"

"Sounds to me like it's best not to choose sides on this one," Aldwyn said. "Perhaps you can share the credit."

"What fun would that be?" Navid asked, as if Aldwyn were crazy for even suggesting such a thing.

"A tie doesn't make two winners," Marati added, clearly in agreement. "It makes two losers."

A spyball descended from above, landing next to the white-tailed mongoose. When Aldwyn was first introduced to the world of magic, he came to know the bat-winged eyeballs as spies for Paksahara. But after her downfall, the spyballs were spared punishment and reemployed by the queens' guard for their original purpose: to alert the protectors of the land to dangers lurking outside the gates of Bronzhaven.

"Looks like there's a disturbance in the east," Marati said. "Navid, I'm afraid it's time for us to go."

"I'll call the Nightfall Battalion," Navid replied.

The two departed, but Aldwyn wasn't left alone for long. He spotted Gilbert sitting on a table across the courtyard. Not surprisingly, his friend was staring dreamily at Anura, the golden toad who was also a part of the circle of heroes. The tree frog had developed a crush on the luck-bringing amphibian, and she didn't seem to mind the attention. Aldwyn approached them.

A worn map was laid flat across the table.

Gilbert's webbed hand gripped a smooth glass stone. He placed it on the map, directly atop Bronzhaven.

"*Locavi instantanus,*" Gilbert incanted. "Show us where the juiciest flies in Vastia reside."

He released his hold on the stone. Suddenly it began to shake and quiver before sliding forward on its own, moving across the map. It stopped at a spot on the map labeled the Urenga Mudlands.

"Huh, I've never even heard of that place," Gilbert said.

"I guess I know where you'll be taking your next vacation," Anura replied.

"Flies never taste as good when you're eating them alone."

"Is that an invitation?" Anura asked playfully.

"That depends. Are you saying yes?"

"What's that you're doing?" Aldwyn interrupted. "With the map."

"I'm locavating," Gilbert replied. "It's one of the knowledge-gathering skills written about in the Protocols of Divination. The Ocean Oracle said it's a sister study of puddle viewing. All you need is a map and an orienteering stone. And a natural talent for seeing beyond the here and now."

"Gilbert, you're telling me you have the ability to locate anything you ask for? Didn't you think that was worth mentioning when I told you I still hadn't found Yeardley?"

"I guess I didn't," Gilbert said. "I can now see how that might have been important to you."

"Well, what are you waiting for?" Aldwyn asked.

"Right!"

Gilbert put the orienteering stone back on Bronzhaven. He focused his energy.

"*Locavi instantanus,*" he said aloud. "Show us the way to the Maidenmere cat called Yeardley."

He removed his hands once more and leaned back expectantly. The stone began to quiver but that's all it did. It never moved.

"Ask it to show you the way to the Well of Ashtheril," Aldwyn said.

"Of course. Yes." Gilbert rested his hand atop the stone and repeated Aldwyn's suggestion. "*Locavi instantanus.* Show us the way to the Well of Ashtheril."

He pulled back and waited. The stone gave an even more dramatic shake. Then it stopped.

Aldwyn's ears, which had perked up with hope, fell.

"I'm sorry, pal," Gilbert said. "Guess I still need some more practice."

"There you two are," Skylar chirped out. "I've been looking everywhere for you!"

Aldwyn and Gilbert turned to see Skylar flying over, carrying a necklace in her talons.

"Come on," she said. "I want us to be the first to give Queen Loranella a gift."

"What did we get her anyway?" Aldwyn asked, looking at the black chain with dangling pearls, their emerald hue glowing under the twinkling light of the floating lanterns.

"It's a necklace," Skylar replied. "I made it myself. These pearls are from some oyster flowers we picked in the Xylem garden. I thought it would be nice for all three of us to present it to her together."

Skylar was about to lead the way, just as one of the floating streamers got caught in a sudden gust of wind and smacked her in the face. Blinded, she flew right into an everwillow tree, causing her to drop the necklace. The chain slid toward a nearby sewer grate.

"Oh, no!" Skylar cried out.

Gilbert made a diving leap, grabbing it moments before it was lost to the tunnels below. Skylar shook free from the tangle of paper and looked to Anura.

"I thought you were supposed to bring luck to everyone *but* Gilbert," she said.

"I can't always explain the nature of my talent," Anura replied. "It continues to surprise even me."

Skylar gave the necklace a quick polish and resumed her flight toward Loranella. Aldwyn and Gilbert followed behind, leaving Anura sitting atop the table with the worn map. The Three arrived to find the queen engaged in a lively discussion with the bearded wizard Urbaugh, her trusted adviser.

"And I respectfully disagree," he said. "A pardon to any who did not stand with you is simply unacceptable. They should be punished as an example to others."

"We're building a new Vastia, one that believes in forgiveness," Loranella replied. "Fear can cloud the soundest mind's judgment."

"And so can generosity," Urbaugh said. "Don't

be naive, my queen. Just because Paksahara is gone does not mean all evil died with her."

Loranella spied Aldwyn, Gilbert, and Skylar waiting nearby.

"We'll continue this later, Urbaugh. Unless I'm mistaken, I thought this was supposed to be a party."

Urbaugh never looked like he was having much fun, but he appeared even more disgruntled than usual. He stomped off and Skylar swooped in.

"Queen Loranella, we've brought you a gift," she said. "It's just a token. Not much really."

"It's beautiful," Loranella said, eyeing the necklace. "In fact, I'd like to try it on right now."

Skylar waved Aldwyn and Gilbert over with a wing. The queen knelt down and lowered her head. Then Aldwyn mentally lifted the chain out of Skylar's grasp and gently guided it around her neck. Loranella glanced at her reflection in the shiny armor of a nearby guard, admiring the gift. The pearls shimmered, making her eyes gleam brighter.

"It's lovely," the queen said. "Thank you."

"I thought you'd like it," Skylar replied, quite

pleased with herself.

"So, now that you've all returned from your questabouts, are you prepared to take the next step in your training?" she asked. "I know Commander Warden expects great things from you. And there is still much for you to . . ."

Loranella's words came to an abrupt stop. She began to gasp for air. Aldwyn watched as the black chain seared itself into the flesh of her neck, and the pearls buried themselves into her chest.

"Skylar, what's happening?" Aldwyn asked in a panic.

"I don't know," she replied, equally alarmed.

"Do something!" Gilbert cried.

But there was nothing they could do. The queen was helpless, too, as the necklace continued to melt into her body. The chain burrowed so deeply under her skin that it appeared to be a thick black vein. The pearls were half-submerged in her collarbone, like seashells sticking out from the sand.

Now others were gathering, shouting out calls for help. The queen dropped down to her knees, and the whites of her eyes turned jet-black.

A palace healer sprinted up with a raven on his shoulder. He pushed aside the familiars as Loranella's lips lost their color.

"Give us some space," the healer ordered.

The raven landed next to the queen and rubbed its feathers across her chest, attempting to use its magical healing talent to cure her. Aldwyn could see that Loranella's breathing had slowed. Her body was stiffening.

Soon, Commander Warden and Sorceress Edna were at the queen's side. Galatea was nearby, as well, clearly upset to see her co-ruler under such severe duress.

"Remove all of her jewelry," the healer said. "I don't want anything interfering with the raven's touch."

Warden pulled off her crown, while Edna removed her rings and bracelets. The raven's wing moved up and down Loranella's arms and across her forehead. But she looked to be slipping ever further toward the Tomorrowlife.

"We need to get her to my chamber," the healer said. "Quickly."

A group of wizards raised their arms and the queen was carried up three stories and into an open window. With his wand outstretched, the palace healer flew behind her, raven at his side.

The enchanted harp had fallen silent. Only panicked muttering could be heard in the still night air. Every eye in the courtyard was on Aldwyn, Skylar, and Gilbert.

Urbaugh and a half-dozen soldiers and wizards surrounded them. Galatea narrowed her eyes.

"Arrest them," she said.

One of the wizards flicked his wrist and

dispeller chains slithered out from the palace
guard shed and wrapped around each of the three
animals' ankles.

"This is a big mistake," Skylar said.

"We would never hurt the queen," Aldwyn
added.

Urbaugh turned to his soldiers.

"Take them to the dungeon," he said coldly.

3

PRISONERS

"What could possibly be taking them so long?" Aldwyn asked. "I don't understand why we're still being kept down here."

Several hours had passed since the familiars had been detained. The steel bars on the dungeon cell stared back at Aldwyn, their dull glow dampening any attempts at magic cast from within. No food. No water. No hint as to what those on the outside had in mind for them.

"We should be out there helping," said Skylar, who was perched on a brick protruding from the wall. "I've seen tomes about reversing those kinds of necromantic spells. The longer we're locked in here, the stronger that curse will become. It could be too late already."

"Let's not overreact, guys," Gilbert said, almost sounding desperate. "The queen is probably recovering as we speak. Urbaugh just hasn't had a chance to release us yet."

"When I find out who's responsible for this, I'll hang the traitor myself," Skylar said.

"Hang?" Gilbert croaked. "Is that what they do to traitors?" He hopped up to the bars and shouted at the top of his lungs, "We're innocent! We didn't do anything!"

"I never met a dungeon dweller who didn't claim to be innocent," a voice called out from the darkness.

Aldwyn looked over to discover that the voice belonged to a warthog standing in the cell across the hall. He was thin and pale, but his tusks appeared as sharp as ever.

"We *are* innocent," Aldwyn said.

"And I did not commit treason against Loranella," the warthog replied, flashing the double hex—two concentric circles with a five-pointed star at its center—branded into his paw.

46

It was the sign of allegiance to Paksahara, the evil hare who had tried to take over the queendom. The warthog continued, "I was trying to save our land from the rule of humans. Good to have the three of you on our side now."

"Are you responsible for this?" Skylar demanded.

The warthog smiled and slunk back into the shadows.

Just then the heavy metal door to the dungeon could be heard swinging open. Footsteps followed and soon a bolka-dur appeared. Troll-like, with green, wart-covered skin and a snout, the creature wore a collar with keys dangling from it. Urbaugh walked alongside the dungeon keeper with a torch floating in front of him. Behind them were three expressionless figures dressed in crimson robes. These were the Truth Seekers, interrogators of the queens' guard. Each removed a steel cage from hooks hanging on the wall and continued down the hall.

The bolka-dur used one of the keys to unlock Aldwyn, Skylar, and Gilbert's cell, and the others entered.

"Galatea has ordered each of you to be questioned," Urbaugh said coldly, avoiding eye contact with the familiars. "And it won't be by me. The Truth Seekers were dragged out in the middle of the night to do it."

"Urbaugh," Aldwyn pleaded, "you know we would never do something like this. Please, you have to believe us."

"In my heart, I do," Urbaugh said. "But what I've seen with my own eyes tells a different story."

Seen with his own eyes? What was he talking about?

Urbaugh gestured for Aldwyn, Skylar, and Gilbert to exit their cell. They were immediately ushered into separate cages, locked in, and picked up by the Truth Seekers. Aldwyn watched through the tiny slit of his cage as he was carried down the hall. He could see other inhabitants of the dungeon staring back at him as he and his companions were led toward the door. Firescale snakes, wolverines, and the worst that humankind had to offer.

"Don't let them intimidate you, brother," one of the wolverines snarled.

"And whatever you do, don't grovel for

forgiveness," added a firescale snake. "You only did what the rest of us wish we could have."

It made Aldwyn's fur bristle to hear these villains of Vastia think of him as one of *them*. He had been thought of as a scoundrel before, when he was forced to steal food on the streets of Bridgetower. But even then, his crimes were committed only so he could survive. He never hurt anyone. Then everything changed for him. Jack chose him as his familiar and he discovered that he was one of the Prophesized Three, destined to save the queendom. He became part of something bigger than himself, something he could be proud of. People saw him not as a lowly street urchin but as a hero. And he never wanted to go back.

The Truth Seekers stopped before the dungeon door, waiting as the bolka-dur let them and Urbaugh through. They continued into the forbidden hallways rarely seen by castle visitors. Aldwyn even caught a glimpse of the steel door to the palace vault, which spit fire as they passed. A few steps later the Truth Seeker carrying Aldwyn took a sudden turn away from Gilbert and Skylar.

"Hey," Aldwyn called. "Where are you taking

me? Why aren't I going with them?"

His questions were met by silence.

Aldwyn's cage was set down on a table and the door unlocked. The Maidenmere cat stepped out and stretched his legs, then looked around the room. It was simple and empty, and the walls were the same creamy alabaster as the ones in the cellar of Kalstaff's cottage.

The Truth Seeker sat opposite him in a chair. The hooded robe was pulled back to reveal a dark-skinned woman, expressionless.

"Ask me anything," Aldwyn said. "I have nothing to hide."

"I will not be the one asking the questions," the woman said. "My familiar will be."

A tarsier emerged from behind her robe. The pocket-size primate had spindly fingers, a snake-like tail three times the length of its body, and giant piercing eyes that took up half its head.

"It's quite a thrill to be sitting across from the prophesized cat," the tarsier said. "And a mighty big surprise. Under these circumstances, anyway."

"Whatever evidence you think you have, it's a setup."

Aldwyn looked into the tarsier's bulging eyes. He attempted to read his mind but was met with nothing more than a hazy cloud of gray. There appeared to be some kind of magic protecting the thoughts of Aldwyn's inquisitor.

"Have you ever been a member of the Noctonati?" the tarsier asked.

"No. Never."

"Have you ever been associated with a member of the Noctonati?"

"What are you getting at?" Aldwyn asked.

"I'll take that as a yes." The tarsier's eyes never wavered from Aldwyn's. "Have you ever been in possession of mugwort? Echo drool? Vulgar cinquefoil?"

"I don't know. I hardly keep track of all the components I've come across."

"Black lichen? Tarantula teeth? Ghoul bile? I could keep going if you like."

"Yes, I'm sure you could," Aldwyn replied. "I just have no idea what it has to do with me."

"They were found in your rooms," the tarsier said. "Along with a copy of *Wyvern and Skull's Tome of the Occult.*"

"That's ridiculous. Someone planted those things," Aldwyn said. "Besides, doesn't that seem a bit convenient? I mean, if I was really going to hurt the queen, why would I leave evidence of it in my room?"

"Ah, so tell me, how *would* you hurt the queen?"

"Now you're just twisting my words," Aldwyn said. "I wouldn't hurt her."

"Whose idea was it to visit Agdaleen's lair?" the tarsier asked.

"That was months ago." Aldwyn thought for a moment. "I suppose it was Skylar."

"Hm. Interesting. And her questabout? Where did she go again?"

"The lost Xylem garden of Horteus Ebekenezer."

"Ah, the fabled garden filled with forbidden components." The tarsier paused. "Have you ever questioned your good friend Skylar's loyalty?"

Aldwyn remained silent. He had.

"Have you ever thought that Skylar was capable of hurting someone that you loved?"

He had.

"I'll take that as a yes."

"But I was wrong," Aldwyn said. "I had misinterpreted one of Gilbert's puddle viewings. I never should have doubted her."

"Or maybe you should have."

"Are you finished yet?" Aldwyn asked.

"No, I'm just getting started. Let's talk about you for a moment. Orphaned as a kitten. A long history of theft. Street fights. There was even a bounty on your head by numerous fish and fowl shops in Bridgetower. They considered you their number one enemy."

"I didn't hear a question."

"Do you ever miss your life of crime?" the tarsier asked.

"No," Aldwyn answered. "Not for a moment. I only did those things out of necessity. To eat. To survive. It's not the same."

"Once a criminal, always a criminal in my book," the tarsier said. "Tell me more. Malvern. He was one of Paksahara's most trusted conspirators. And your uncle."

"Malvern betrayed me and my family. I was hardly on his side. His death at my paw should be evidence enough of that."

"So you admit that you *are* a murderer?"

"It was self-defense," Aldwyn said.

"But you proved that you're capable of killing."

Aldwyn was getting more and more frustrated. He didn't like this one bit. And even though it was tempting, clawing the tarsier's eyes out certainly wouldn't help his cause.

"You haven't even told me," Aldwyn said, holding back his anger. "How is Queen Loranella?"

"Concerned that perhaps you and your companions didn't finish the job?"

"Please," Aldwyn said. "Please tell me that she's all right."

"The best healers in Vastia are by her side. They've been able to keep her in the Wander, between this life and the Tomorrowlife."

Aldwyn exhaled. Relief flooded him. No matter the predicament he was in, at least she wasn't dead.

The door creaked open and one of the other crimson-robed Truth Seekers entered. She walked up to the woman sitting across from Aldwyn and whispered in her ear. As suddenly as she arrived, she was gone.

"Gilbert has confessed," said the woman. "This interrogation does not need to go on any longer."

"It's a lie," Aldwyn said. "I don't believe it."

"Perhaps his conscience was heavier than yours," the tarsier said.

"No. You must have confused him. Or tricked him. There was nothing for him to admit to, because we didn't do anything!"

"This much I do know," the tarsier said. "There will be leniency for those who cooperate. If you insist on withholding the truth, your punishment will be severe."

No threat, whatever the consequence, would make the orphan cat confess to a crime he didn't commit. Growing up on the streets of Bridgetower, honor was all that he had. And he wasn't going to compromise it now.

"I'm innocent," Aldwyn said simply. "We all are."

The tarsier turned to his loyal and the two shared a look.

"Back in your cage, cat," the Truth Seeker said.

Aldwyn returned to the metal carrier. The tarsier climbed inside his loyal's robe, and she locked the cage and lifted it from the table.

She retraced her steps back to the door of the dungeon, where the bolka-dur was waiting. The creature gleefully ran his stubby fingers along the chain of keys around his neck until he found the right one and slid it into the lock. Once through to the other side, they returned to Aldwyn's cell, where again the bolka-dur did what he did best. He unlocked the otherwise impenetrable cell. Gilbert was already inside.

Aldwyn's cage door was opened and he was allowed to join his companion. The Truth Seeker departed. Gilbert sat in the corner, a mix of shock and fear on his face.

"They said they have evidence, Aldwyn," Gilbert croaked. "Components, hexes, diaries filled with our plans."

"Someone obviously wants us to take the fall for this," Aldwyn replied. "The question is who."

"The palace chef has had it out for me ever since I criticized his beetle soup."

"I think this might be a little more complicated than that," Aldwyn said.

Aldwyn's mind was racing through the

possibilities. There were the strangers he had met at the celebration. Then there were the animals who remained loyal to Paksahara but still were unaccounted for. And the humans who never liked the decision made by Loranella to share her throne with Galatea. That hardly narrowed it down.

Just then, something on the ground caught Aldwyn's eye. A line was being drawn in the dust and grime clinging to the stone floor, as if an invisible finger was moving just below the surface. At first Aldwyn figured it was nothing more than a phantom slug. But after a moment he realized that letters were being written, from right to left. Already **woyt** had been spelled, and the letters were coming faster now. Just to the left of the **w** came a **d**, then **s**, **o**, and **u**. The finished word spelled **uosdwoyt**.

"Gilbert, come look at this," Aldwyn said.

The tree frog hopped over to Aldwyn's side and looked down at the floor. A second word had already formed to the left of the first: **udpjbm**.

"Udpjbm uosdwoyt?" Gilbert asked. "What does it mean? I don't get it."

"Neither do I," Aldwyn replied.

"You mean you're not using your telekinesis to do that?"

"No."

More words were forming in the dirt. Aldwyn and Gilbert just stood there watching until whatever was writing them was done. Then Aldwyn read the words aloud:

"Spuowbip wjots sby udpjbm uosdwoyt. I think it's some kind of message for us."

"But who from?" Gilbert asked.

"I don't know. Another prisoner or a spirit from the Tomorrowlife? The castle itself. It could be anyone."

"Well, whoever sent it must think we speak gobbledygook," Gilbert said. "Because that doesn't make any sense."

Down the hall they saw another Truth Seeker carrying Skylar to the cell. The bolka-dur unlocked the door and the blue jay fluttered out from the cage to perch again on the protruding brick. The dungeon keeper slammed the cell door shut once more, relocking it. The bolka-dur then followed the Truth Seeker toward the dungeon exit, where she placed the open cage back on its hook before being led outside.

"You okay?" Aldwyn asked Skylar.

She didn't respond.

"Well, you got back just in time," he continued. "I think somebody's trying to tell us something."

Again, she just sat there quietly.

"Come on, Skylar, I need you to look at this," Aldwyn said, growing impatient. "It's written in some other language."

"What's wrong with her?" Gilbert asked.

Then, before their eyes, the blue jay vanished.

By the time Aldwyn and Gilbert realized what had happened, Skylar had flown out from the cage hanging down the hall and was hovering just outside their locked cell door. She had tricked them all with a clever illusion. The real Skylar had been in the cage the whole time.

"We have to hurry," she said. "The dungeon keeper will be back shortly."

"How are you going to get us out?" Gilbert asked. "He has the only key that can unlock this door."

"Not the only one," she said.

Skylar raised her wings and focused on the keyhole.

"What are you doing?" Aldwyn asked.

"Remember what Hepsibah was able to do over Liveod's Canyon?" Skylar replied. "The most powerful birds at Nearhurst can create illusions so convincing that they can momentarily take solid form."

"I thought only five-feather master illusionists could do that," Gilbert said.

"Well, I've been practicing. Now be quiet. I

need to find my focal point."

She concentrated and soon a key began to materialize. Aldwyn did a double take. He couldn't believe it wasn't real. The key found its way into the lock and gave a twist. Then the cell door opened.

"Wait," Aldwyn said. "Before we go, there's something you need to see. A message, written on the floor of our cell. It just appeared out of nowhere."

Skylar glanced over and repeated the strange words aloud.

"Come on," Skylar said. "I've already memorized it. We'll figure it out later. Now let's go."

As the three animals took to the hall, prisoners from the neighboring cells ran up to their bars making a racket.

"Hey, let us out, too!" a pockmarked man with no teeth shouted.

"I don't belong in here," an elvin pirate called.

"I'll help you escape," the firescale snake hissed from a cell with bars so tight even she couldn't slip through.

"You're not going to leave without us, are you,

brother?" the wolverine called out to Aldwyn.

"I'm not your brother," Aldwyn yelled back.

The familiars hurried for the dungeon door. But they'd made it only halfway there when the bolka-dur burst through, spiked billy club in hand.

"Shut your slop holes," he hollered, banging his club against the first bars he could. Then his eyes fell on Aldwyn, Skylar, and Gilbert running toward him. "How did you? It's impossible."

He flung his spiked billy club down the hall like an ax. Aldwyn used his telekinesis to catch it in midair, then fired it back at the dungeon keeper. The blunt end struck the bolka-dur square in the forehead, knocking him out cold. His body dropped to the stone floor, his head landing against the bars of one of the cells.

The familiars were now racing toward an open door. But no escape plan could go that smoothly. A wrinkled hand reached out through the cell bars and a witch's fingernail sliced through the band of the bolka-dur's leather collar. She lifted the key ring off his neck and unlocked the door to her dungeon cell.

Reveling in her first taste of freedom, the witch threw the key ring into the air and incanted: *"Otebrit vsechny dvere!"*

And with those words uttered, the keys broke off from the chain and soared through the air, until each one found its home in a different lock. Then the keys turned in unison, opening every last cell door in the dungeon block. Prisoners poured out into the hall. With a mob mentality, they turned on the fallen bolka-dur.

Aldwyn came to a stop at the door.

"Come on," Skylar urged. "This is our chance. Let's go."

But Aldwyn couldn't just let the dungeon keeper get ripped to pieces. He eyed the spiked billy club and telekinetically lifted it from the ground, swinging it in a circle around the bolka-dur to ward off any attackers.

Skylar and Gilbert reluctantly turned back to help.

Suddenly a dozen palace guards were rushing through the dungeon door, drawing the attention of the prisoners. Aldwyn could tell by the way Skylar was holding her wing that these were mere

illusions. He immediately focused all his mental energy on the bolka-dur and strained to tug him across the floor with his mind.

All through the dungeon there was chaos. Bolts flew from the witch's fingertips and flames blasted off the back of the firescale snake. Aldwyn was even nearly gouged by the sharpened tusk of the warthog.

The familiars were able to escape through the dungeon door, dragging the bolka-dur behind them. The elvin pirate tried to slip through as well, but Gilbert bounced up and kicked him, forcing him to stumble backward. Aldwyn tele-kinetically slammed the door shut and sent the blockade bar crashing down across it. Leaving the still unconscious bolka-dur resting against the door, the trio continued on their way.

They had successfully fled the dungeon, but they still had to navigate their way out of the castle and escape the city. The familiars had gone from being Vastia's most celebrated to its most wanted.

The Prophesized Three were fugitives.

4

ICARI WEED

"This is the way they led us in," Skylar said, soaring up to the base of a staircase.

"Then that's definitely not the way we want to go out," Aldwyn said. "There must be other passageways, ones that are less traveled."

Aldwyn bounded down the hall, passing by the palace vault once more. Multiple corridors split off from the main stretch, each one looking identical.

"Over here," Aldwyn said, starting down one of the passages.

Gilbert came to a halt.

"Now doesn't seem like the best time for guessing," he said.

"I'm not. I smell fish."

Gilbert and Skylar followed him, and sure enough, they came to another set of stairs leading upward. Aldwyn began climbing, with his companions right behind him. They ascended three flights before emerging into the palace kitchen.

Aldwyn had sneaked through many a cooking quarter in his day, from the tiny ones in the fishmonger shops in Bridgetower to the magically endowed one in Sorceress Edna's Black Ivy Manor. But never had he been inside a kitchen as enormous as this. Had it been any other day, he would have explored every pantry and ice chest. Now he had to resist even the fillet of salmon cooking over the nearby fire.

The kitchen staff tended to different pots and pans, while the palace chef barked orders and dipped his finger in a stew for a taste. The familiars tiptoed across the floor and exited into the dining hall, where an informal buffet was being served for those keeping an all-night vigil for the queen. Few of those gathered seemed to have much of an appetite, instead poking worriedly at platefuls of food with their forks.

Skylar landed on Aldwyn's back and beckoned Gilbert to join her. Once they were both aboard, Skylar waved a wing and Aldwyn could see in a mirrored wall that the three of them now appeared to be one of the many palace bulldogs that roamed the halls. As they walked through the room, Aldwyn could hear snippets of talk from those gathered around the table.

"I hear that her heart is beating once every five minutes. And that her fingertips are cold enough to make water freeze."

"Few wake from the Wander. Without the right counterspell, she may remain trapped there for eternity."

"What's the alternative? The Tomorrowlife?"

Aldwyn slowed his pace to hear more.

"Do you know if those without magic are allowed to join the wizards seeking out that spell?"

"I'm sure Galatea would welcome any volunteers."

"There are already dozens of scholars poring over every text in the queen's library. But her personal collection is limited. The most ancient spell books were destroyed when the Historical

Archives were eaten by those bookworms."

"Perhaps that was all part of the familiars' plan."

Those assembled nodded their heads in agreement. How quickly these lies had poisoned their reputation. Aldwyn gnashed his teeth angrily.

Once he reached the other side of the room, Aldwyn slipped into the hallway. With Skylar maintaining the illusion, Aldwyn started toward the grand foyer.

"We won't survive for long out there without supplies," Skylar said. "I need my satchel."

"Once the bolka-dur comes to, he's going to realize we're gone, and every last person in this palace will be hunting us down," Aldwyn said. "You really want to take that risk?"

"I don't think he'll be waking up anytime soon," Skylar said. "And by the time he does, we'll be long gone."

Aldwyn turned for the palace staircase and climbed to the top, where his paws touched the soft velvet carpeting that covered every floor on the second level. The familiars' rooms were at the far side of the hall, by the northern tower. To get there, they would have to walk directly past

Queen Loranella's chambers.

The temptation to run was great, but Aldwyn knew that a sprinting bulldog was sure to draw attention. So he kept a steady pace, fighting every instinct he had for urgency.

As they walked, an old man pushing a cart filled with vials and potions passed them. He had a solemn look on his tattooed face. Aldwyn recognized the markings as those of the driftfolk. The glass beakers and goblets churned and gurgled, as if the multicolored brews within might bubble out at any moment. Aldwyn looked ahead and realized the man had come from Loranella's room. Outside her door, a group of ravens and healers were gathered, all talking in hushed tones as they watched the old man depart.

"That didn't do any good," one of the healers said.

"What did you expect?" a raven asked. "He was a driftfolk charlatan. Half those potions were probably colored with beet juice."

"Then what was he doing here?" another raven asked.

"We're desperate," the healer said. "The

parasitic poison is spreading faster than we can contain it."

"Well, if we don't figure out something, I won't be able to keep her in the Wander for more than two, maybe three days," the first raven replied.

"An aardvark is on the way," a second healer interjected. "Hopes to reverse the curse using mud from the bottom of the Time Stream."

"We really are desperate," the second raven said.

Aldwyn slowed as he passed the queen's chambers. The door had been left open a sliver. Beneath the canopy of the large bed he could see Loranella. It looked like she was sleeping, but Aldwyn knew this was a sleep few ever awoke from.

A pair of Sun Temple worshippers knelt on mats placed by the window. They dropped flower petals into a bronze offering bowl sitting between them. Dawn was still a few hours away, but they wanted to be ready for the day's first rays of sun. Aldwyn only hoped that their prayers would be answered.

Anura sat on the pillow beside Loranella. The golden toad stroked the queen's white hair tenderly. Anura's good luck hadn't brought Loranella back to life, but maybe it was all that was keeping her from already being dead.

Aldwyn heard Gilbert sniffle.

"I'm sorry," he whispered, trying not to cry. "I just hate to see her like this."

"So do we," Skylar assured him. "But we need to keep moving."

Aldwyn knew she was right and continued to Skylar's room. A soldier stood at the door, presumably to make certain that no evidence inside was tampered with. Aldwyn kept walking.

"In here," Skylar said, giving Aldwyn's ear a little tug to the left.

He followed her none-too-subtle instruction, darting into a parlor two doors down from her room. Skylar lowered her wings and let the illusion disappear.

"We won't be able to get past the guard," she said. "I'll have to go in through the window."

Aldwyn saw that there was a window on the opposite side of the parlor, and Skylar was already flapping toward it.

"Wait here," she said. "I'll be right back."

With that, she flew out of the parlor. Aldwyn

and Gilbert stayed behind, trying to remain as quiet as possible. Tomes were piled up atop a reading desk with titles on the spines reading *Remedies for Every Malady, Astraloch's A-to-Z Guide to Antidotes,* and *Porkivit's Potion Primer.*

"Maybe the answer to the queen's ailment is in one of those books," Gilbert said, hopping onto the desk.

"Gilbert, stay away from—" Aldwyn started to say, but it was too late.

The tree frog had already flipped open one of the tomes, and as soon as he did, all the candles in the room flickered on and the organ in the corner began to play quiet, melodic music.

"The parlor is enchanted with mood magic," Aldwyn said.

It was very pleasant for quiet study, but not good for hiding out. Gilbert slammed the book shut, but that didn't stop the music.

"Get off the reading desk," Aldwyn called.

Gilbert quickly jumped down and the organ silenced itself. The flames burning on the candles extinguished themselves. Aldwyn and Gilbert stood still, as if their silence would erase the noise that had just filled the room. They listened anxiously, waiting to see if they had drawn anyone's attention. Then the doorknob began to turn.

"Window," Aldwyn said, running for the other side of the parlor.

Gilbert leaped behind him, and the two took to the ledge outside. Just as they pressed their backs to the palace wall, Aldwyn could hear someone enter the room. The heavy thud of boots pounding across the floor got closer.

Still clinging to the ledge thirty feet above the courtyard, Aldwyn watched as Skylar flew from her bedroom window with her leather satchel slung over her wing.

"What are you doing?" she asked. "I told you to wait inside."

Then she heard the boot steps coming from the parlor. The Three froze, not daring to make the slightest sound. Aldwyn was practically holding his breath, until the noise faded and they heard the door close.

They all exhaled.

"Guys, look," Gilbert said, pointing down below.

Aldwyn could see Navid, Marati, and the rest of the Nightfall Battalion entering through the gate. The men, women, and animals wore black armor with faint silhouettes of the stars and moon on the shoulders. It appeared the assassination attempt on Queen Loranella had taken precedence over whatever mission they had been called to. In their short existence, the Nightfall Battalion had quickly become the stuff of legend. They had hunted and apprehended dozens of Paksahara's most loyal followers, traitors to the queendom who had gone on the run after the Dead Army's fall. Most of the prisoners filling the dungeon below the palace had been caught in their nets. Now Aldwyn, Skylar, and Gilbert were their targets.

Fortunately, none of them was looking up. At least not yet.

Aldwyn eyed the dozens of paper lanterns floating in the air, calculating the space between them. They led across to a wall with a staircase winding down to the courtyard.

"We should be able to make it across on those lanterns," Aldwyn said.

"It will be just like hopping lily pads back home," Gilbert said.

"Or rooftops," Aldwyn added.

Skylar seemed to be on board with the plan, as she was already flying ahead. Then Gilbert was off, making the first two jumps effortlessly. Aldwyn leaped from the ledge next, his paws touching down on the paper lantern closest to him. It cracked under his feet, but before it gave way he bounded again.

Aldwyn quickened, jumping across three more lanterns. Gilbert continued to set the pace out front. But just as the tree frog landed on the next lantern, the paper split in half. Gilbert narrowly made it off in time, just before the lantern debris scattered to the ground.

Aldwyn was now staring ahead at a six-foot gap. He didn't have time to think about it, though. He simply had to keep moving. And that's just what he did, jumping through the air to the next lantern. His front paws nearly slipped upon making contact, but his claws took hold and he was able to pull himself to safety. Aldwyn made one more leap and joined Gilbert and Skylar on the ledge of the outer wall.

Skylar flew above the courtyard and glanced down.

"It's clear," she said.

Aldwyn and Gilbert sprinted down the staircase, until they reached the ground. Skylar fluttered to their side. Party decorations, half-eaten plates of food, and a table filled with unopened gifts all remained untouched, evidence of a celebration cut short. The three familiars quickly passed the golden eel pond and headed for the front gate.

"Wait up," Gilbert said.

Hopping over to the table where he and Anura had been sitting during the queen's birthday festivities, he grabbed his orienteering stone and cloth map.

"Thought these might come in handy," Gilbert said, hurrying to catch back up with Aldwyn and Skylar while slinging the map's tie string over his shoulder.

Aldwyn wasn't so sure the map would help, seeing how Gilbert failed to find Yeardley. But he'd already taken it, so there was no point leaving it behind now.

The familiars were halfway across the courtyard

when the tower bell started clanging.

"They know we've escaped," Skylar said.

Aldwyn and Gilbert began to sprint, but the front gate was already swinging shut. Even at top running speed, Aldwyn knew he wasn't going to make it. He turned to a nearby dining chair on the courtyard patio and telekinetically flung it into the path of the closing gate. The force of the steel door was too much for the metal chair to hold, and it snapped in two as the gate closed completely.

The three animals had to change direction. They turned back to see Navid and Marati emerging from the palace with a dozen soldiers of the Nightfall Battalion. The familiars were being surrounded.

"Surrender now," Marati called out. "There's nowhere for you to go."

"We fought side by side," Aldwyn said. "Practically stood together in the circle of heroes. Why would we do something like this? It doesn't make any sense."

"It's not my job to decide if you're innocent or guilty," Marati replied. "But I know we can't let you run away."

"Navid, we're friends," Gilbert said. "Please."

"I'm sorry. There's nothing I can do."

Aldwyn hadn't noticed until now, but Skylar was removing something from her satchel.

"Eat this," she whispered, handing prickly blades of grass to both Aldwyn and Gilbert. "Trust me."

The two immediately swallowed them. The soldiers were now tightening their circle around the trio with swords drawn. Navid bared his fangs, and Aldwyn knew all too well the powerful venom blasts he was capable of shooting from them. Marati had already summoned her astral claws, sharp blue glowing blades commanded by the mongoose.

Suddenly Aldwyn felt a throbbing below his shoulders. It made him wince.

"What did you just give me?" he asked Skylar.

"Icari weed," she replied.

Aldwyn searched his memory. He had heard that component mentioned once before, but he couldn't remember when.

"Remind me what that does agahhhhhhh . . ." Pressure was building up and then a searing pain rocketed along Aldwyn's spine. It was like a pair of knives had been stabbed through his back. As quickly as the shock of pain had rattled him, it was gone. Gilbert was writhing as well. Then Aldwyn realized that something was starting to poke out from the tree frog's back. They were slimy, bat-like wings! Aldwyn glanced around to see that he, too, was growing wings of his own, but unlike Gilbert's, they were covered in the black-and-white fur of a Maidenmere cat.

"Fly!" Skylar shouted.

Although Aldwyn had never sprouted wings before, his body seemed to know just what to do. Muscles began contracting and expanding, and the wings on his back flapped. He was up off the ground. And Gilbert was right beside him.

"Get back here!" Marati cried.

It was too late for that. The familiars were soaring skyward. Navid fired a venom blast but it fell short. Marati's astral claw was immediately weakened by the distance it had to travel.

"After them!" Navid shouted from below.

Aldwyn turned his attention to the clouds before him. The Icari weed had taken effect so quickly he'd barely had time to process it. But this would

not be the moment to reflect, as a half-dozen members of the Nightfall Battalion were flying through the air behind them with wands outstretched. The fastest two caught up to Aldwyn and Gilbert in mere seconds. They were about to ensnare them with golden lassos.

"Creeping vine, possum tail, make them move like a snail!" Gilbert incanted.

Suddenly the two wizards slowed to a near crawl. They tried to talk but even their lips appeared to move in slow motion.

"Quick thinking, Gilbert," Skylar said.

"A snail spell," the tree frog replied. "One of Marianne's favorites."

"Well, she would be proud," Aldwyn said.

Gilbert had little time to bask in the praise, as more members of the Nightfall Battalion were gaining on them.

Aldwyn remembered some flight tactics from *Crady's Book of Aerial Wizardry*, a text he had studied back at Black Ivy Manor. He was just hoping that some of them would be helpful here.

Aldwyn spotted the floating torches that always stood high above the castle walls. But rather than avoiding the bright-glowing flames, he began flapping toward them. Skylar and Gilbert did the same, and the three slalomed between them. The closest pursuing member of the Nightfall Battalion hit the first torch, accidentally setting his robe on fire and forcing him to retreat. The three animals continued to execute hairpin turns and mid-flight reversals that would have made Crady himself proud. Their impressive aerial acrobatics led one of the three remaining Nightfall Battalion soldiers to veer headfirst into the parapet of the palace's high tower.

Aldwyn, Skylar, and Gilbert cleared the outer wall of the castle and were soaring over the city. A searing white blast shot past Aldwyn's head. If he hadn't already had a chunk missing from his ear, he would have now. Aldwyn glanced back to see the last two Nightfall Battalion members charging, both with wands outstretched, one's tip still smoking. Skylar and Gilbert joined Aldwyn as he dipped down a busy street, the buildings towering like canyon walls on either side. They were zipping underneath canopies. Vendors stared up at the strange sight of a cat, frog, and blue jay flying through the air.

Another bolt of lightning came close to frying Gilbert. Aldwyn focused his mind as he passed over the next building, telekinetically pulling shingles from the slanted wooden rooftop and flinging them backward like diamond throwing stars. The barrage of projectiles hit the last two Nightfall Battalion soldiers, knocking their wands from their hands. They instantly began to plummet, heading straight for the pavement. But before they made impact, Aldwyn glanced down and moved a vendor's hay cart with his mind, setting it directly in their path.

Escape seemed within reach. That's when Aldwyn saw a furry black-and-white feather drift from his back. Then another. And another. He was losing his wings. The Icari weed was wearing off. He looked over to Gilbert and saw that his slimy bat wings were beginning to break apart as well.

"Skylar," Aldwyn called out. "You have any more of that Icari weed in your satchel?"

"That was all of it," she replied.

Aldwyn surveyed the cityscape before them.

The outer ring of Bronzhaven was filled with modest residential houses and small parks with well-trimmed lawns and absolutely nowhere to hide. Farther ahead was an orchard of trees and thick bushes.

"Over there," Skylar said, pointing to the orchard. "It will cushion your fall."

It seemed as good a plan as any, except Gilbert was never going to make it. One of his wings had fallen off and he was spiraling downward. He was trying his best to stay afloat, but it was only resulting in an awkward nosedive.

Gilbert's touchdown was bumpy to say the least, but it didn't seem to leave any permanent damage. Aldwyn dropped to the grass feet first, as cats have a tendency to do. Skylar hovered above them.

"More of the Nightfall Battalion will be coming," Skylar said.

"We should go to Turnbuckle Academy and find our loyals," Gilbert said. "They'll be able to help us."

"No," Skylar was quick to respond. "We can't put them at risk. If they appear to be accomplices, they'll be in as much trouble as we are. Besides, our first priority is saving Queen Loranella."

"And how exactly do we plan on doing that?" Aldwyn asked.

"There are only a few in Vastia who know how to cure a parasitic poison," Skylar replied. "But just one is far enough removed from the politics of the palace to be trusted. The Mountain Alchemist in Kailasa."

"He wasn't exactly welcoming the last time we went to him for help," Gilbert croaked.

"He did come through for us, though," Skylar countered.

"Yeah, after he nearly killed us!" Gilbert exclaimed. "And I seem to remember him telling us never to come back to see him again."

"I don't know what other choice we have," Skylar replied. "If we head south, to the forest surrounding the Smuggler's Trail, its magic will keep us hidden from anyone who comes looking for us. Then we can continue on to Kailasa."

Aldwyn turned back and took one last look at the palace. He knew they wouldn't be able to return until they had cleared their names.

5

GAME OF SLUGGOTS

In the morning sunlight, sheep grazed peacefully across the plains east of the Smuggler's Trail. They were of little interest to the spyballs flying above. Which is precisely why Aldwyn, Gilbert, and Skylar had spent the last few hours hidden among them, disguised beneath one of Skylar's illusions. And although this gave them safe cover, it also slowed them down.

"All they eat is grass?" Gilbert asked. "That's it. Every meal. Grass!"

"You pretty much just eat bugs," Aldwyn said.

"But there are so many different varieties. Caterbeetles for the hearty meat lover. The delicate sweetness of a mosquitoette. Or the earthy zest of a dung roach. I could go on."

"That's okay," Aldwyn said.

"When that flock of spyballs soars past, I say we make a break for the edge of the forest," Skylar said.

They waited until the winged eyeballs completed their flyover and disappeared into a low cloud bank. Once they were gone, Aldwyn—with Skylar and Gilbert sitting atop his back—split off from the herd, eager to slip under the thick brush of leaves and branches.

Inside the woods it was cool and quiet, and it took only a few steps to feel like the fields behind them were miles away. Now safely hidden, Skylar dispelled the illusion.

"If we keep moving in this direction, we should come across the Smuggler's Trail," Skylar said.

"We still haven't talked about what was written on the floor of our dungeon cell," Aldwyn said as the group continued onward. "What if it was a clue?"

"Spuowbip wjots sby udpjbm uosdwoyt," Skylar recited from memory.

"How do you *do* that?" Gilbert asked, impressed even though he had seen Skylar's perfect recall on display many times before.

"I'm not sure what the words mean," Skylar continued. "Could be elvish. It also sounds like the ancient tongue of the driftfolk."

"I don't think I mentioned it before, but when the words formed, they were written backward, from right to left," Aldwyn said.

"That's how the elvish script their sentences," Skylar said. "Perhaps along the way to Kailasa we can find someone to help us translate it. Or maybe the Alchemist can do it himself."

As the familiars walked deeper into the forest, Aldwyn could sense that they were not alone. But each time he turned, all he heard was the faint rustling of leaves. He remembered the last time he had traveled here and how this enchanted place hid things right before its visitors' very eyes.

Skylar led them farther still, until they came to a well-worn dirt path. This was the Smuggler's Trail. Hoof marks and dry leaves covered the road.

"Let's lie low for a few hours," Skylar said. "Like

I said, whoever comes looking for us won't be able to find us here."

She gestured to an oak tree that provided ample cover. The Three walked beneath it and started to settle in. But just before Aldwyn got comfortable, he spied a gathering beyond the oak, one he hadn't seen before. Humans, animals, and magical creatures of every kind crowded the grounds. Wooden shelters built into the tree trunks and tents made from old linens and tapestries encircled a campfire. Trolls and fairies sat side by side before the flames. A pair of tiny hippopotamuses were bartering with a slithering mound of moss.

Skylar and Gilbert were now standing beside Aldwyn, staring at the sight.

One of the fairies, who was broad-shouldered and bearded, flitted over and landed on a twig near Aldwyn's face.

"Welcome," he said. "If you can see us, then you must be hiding from something as well. The Smuggler's Den only reveals itself to those who wish not to be found. No one will ask you any questions about what you're running away from here. And as long as you mean no harm to the others, you can stay as long as you like."

"We won't be long," Skylar said.

"Well, if you're hungry, we were just putting some coconut meat over the fire," the fairy said.

"We do have a big day ahead of us," Skylar said.

"Of course, you'll have to contribute something in return," the fairy said.

"And what exactly did you have in mind?" Skylar asked.

The familiars, with bellies filled, scrubbed a stack of pots and pans that stretched halfway up a tree, using wet rags and sticks to clean the grimy cookware. It seemed a fair trade-off, especially since they didn't know where their next full meal was going to come from.

Nearby a gold-backed baboon with a shackle still dangling from one of its wrists tended to the campfire, ensuring that the cooking flames would continue to burn until their next meal. He glanced over to Aldwyn, Skylar, and Gilbert.

"Some of these people have been here so long they don't recognize you," the baboon said. "Not me. I've seen the statues they erected in Split

River. I know it's impolite to ask, but what are the Prophesized Three doing here?"

"It's just a big misunderstanding actually," Skylar said.

"Whatever it is, it must be pretty bad for you to be here," the baboon replied.

"No matter," Skylar said. "It will all be righted soon."

"Righted, perhaps," the baboon said. "But not forgotten. Accusations, whether they be true or false, are not washed out so easily. It takes more than truth to clean the stains that are left behind."

It was as if the baboon knew Aldwyn's worst fear.

"You can do a thousand good acts, but they'll remember you for the one bad. Even if it's just rumor and innuendo."

"That doesn't seem fair, does it?" Aldwyn asked.

"No, I suppose not," the baboon replied.

Aldwyn reflected on everything he and his friends had already been through. He wasn't going to let one false accusation wipe away all the good they had done.

"What about you?" Gilbert asked. "What's with the shackle?"

The baboon stoked the flames again.

"I was taken from my family and sold into the service of the Cyrus Brothers Traveling Animal Show," he said angrily. Aldwyn knew how hard it was to be separated from family. That's why he was so eager to find Yeardley—once all this was over, of course. "They chained me up pretty tight, too. They wanted me to dance for peanuts. But I learned a few tricks from the troop's master escapist, a land octopus who goes by the name Torgo. Thought I'd hide here for a few months."

The fairy returned when the washup was done.

"Same deal goes for lunch," he said.

Aldwyn, Skylar, and Gilbert set down their dishrags and sticks. They'd started back for the tree they planned to lie low beneath when they heard cheers and curses coming from a motley crew of ruffians gathered nearby. Curious, the Three stopped to look closer.

A bull's-eye had been nailed to a tree, and each player stood about ten feet away, throwing their own uniquely striped slug at the target.

"Is that darts?" Gilbert asked.

"Those don't look like darts to me," Aldwyn replied.

Unlike the traditional version of the game, the slugs moved after they made contact, sometimes inching closer to the center, sometimes squirming farther away. If one of the slugs got too close to the other, they would fight until one was swallowed. Once everyone had taken their turn, the player with the slug nearest to the bull's-eye was declared the victor.

"I win," a long-armed sloth exclaimed.

She collected the pile of loot that had been wagered. The others appeared downright livid.

"Look," Skylar said quietly to Aldwyn and Gilbert. "A pair of elvin pirates."

"We'll definitely want to steer clear of them," Gilbert said.

"No," Skylar replied. "They speak elvish. And they'll be able to read elvish."

"And you're going where with this?" Gilbert asked.

"The clue on the dungeon floor," Aldwyn said, jumping in.

"Ah. Yes. The clue." Gilbert nodded.

Skylar and Aldwyn shared an exasperated look.

"Let's see if we can't ask for their help," Skylar said.

The familiars approached the two elvin pirates, one of whom was covering a slug in his own spit.

"I said lightly drooled, Scoot. Too much saliva makes them wobble."

"Brinn, if you don't like the way I spittle your sluggot, do it yourself."

"Excuse us," Skylar said. "We were wondering if we might ask you a favor?"

"Pirates aren't in the business of doing favors," Brinn replied. "We do things for gold and cider."

"Well, we have nothing to offer," Skylar said.

"Then take your wings and beak and flap off," he said.

"We'd be willing to make you a wager," Aldwyn said.

The pirates' eyes lit up. Now Aldwyn had their attention.

"You want to challenge us to a game of slug-gots?" Scoot asked. "Did you hear that, Brinn? Sounds like a bet."

"It sure does," Brinn replied with a grin. "So, what exactly are we playing for?"

"If we win, information," Aldwyn said.

"And if I win?" Brinn asked.

Aldwyn clearly hadn't thought that far in advance. He looked over to the oak tree and spotted Skylar's leather satchel.

"We've got a satchel filled with rare components from Horteus Ebekenezer's lost Xylem garden," Aldwyn said. "You can take your pick of one."

"I want the whole bag," Brinn said. "And the frog, too."

Gilbert croaked. "Guess we'll need a new plan—"

"Deal," Aldwyn said.

Skylar seemed just as surprised as Gilbert.

"Who's throwing for you?" Scoot asked.

Skylar held up her wings.

"I won't be a very good shot with these feathers."

"And my paws will fare no better," Aldwyn said.

They both looked to Gilbert.

"Me?" he asked. "I'm nervous enough as it is."

"Don't worry, buddy," Aldwyn said. "You'll do fine."

"Get yourself a sluggot out of the bucket," Scoot said.

The rest of the ruffians had stepped aside to watch. Brinn was already standing by the line drawn in the dirt. Gilbert stuck a webbed hand into the slug pail and removed one of the slimy critters.

"I'll go first," Brinn said.

He took aim at the bull's-eye, squeezing the sluggot between his fingers. He drew his hand back and fired. The slug tumbled through the air, making a hideous smacking sound as it hit the target. It was high and outside, but after a moment, the creature began to move, squirming its way toward the center. It stopped just short of the innermost ring.

Brinn's toss did nothing to calm Gilbert's nerves. The tree frog stepped up next. The slug was desperately trying to slither out of his grasp.

"Look on the bright side, little guy," Gilbert said. "If I wasn't about to throw you, I'd probably be eating you."

Gilbert swung back his arm and flung the slug-got into the air. It went flying. Aldwyn could see that it was veering off course, so he gave it a little nudge with his telekinesis. Maybe it was cheating, but the queen's life was on the line. And time wasn't exactly on their side. The slug hit the bull's-eye. There were gasps from the spectators. Scoot and Brinn couldn't believe it. Neither could Gilbert or Skylar.

"Move, sluggot!" Brinn shouted.

Gilbert's slug looked like it was ready to make a slow dash for the other end of the target. But Aldwyn wasn't going to let that happen. He took mental hold of the critter's rear and held it in place. After a bit of struggle, the sluggot gave up.

"We have a winner," the long-armed sloth declared.

Brinn slapped Scoot across the back of his head.

"I told you it was too much saliva!"

"I don't know what happened," Scoot replied sheepishly.

Aldwyn and Skylar came up on either side of Gilbert and gave him pats on the back.

"Beginner's luck, I guess," Gilbert said.

"Must have been," Aldwyn said.

The Three walked over to Brinn to collect on their bet.

"So what is it that you want to know?" he asked bitterly. "I don't know nothing about any treasure. And if I did, I can't promise I'd be honorable."

"It has nothing to do with that," Skylar said. "Spuowbip wjots sby udpjbm uosdwoyt. Does that mean anything to you?"

"Sounds like gibberish if you ask me," he replied.

"That's not elvish?" Skylar asked.

"None that I've ever heard."

"Perhaps I'm not pronouncing it correctly,"

Skylar said. "First word is spelled s-p-u-o-w-b-i-p."

"Nothing," Brinn said.

"And how do we know you're being honorable?" Aldwyn asked.

"I have no riches to lose on this one," he said. "I promise you, it's nothing I've ever heard before. And my mother yelled at me in every elvish dialect there is."

Aldwyn, Skylar, and Gilbert began to walk away.

"I knew it was a long shot," Skylar said. "But at least we've ruled it out."

"Hey, frog, what's your secret?" Brinn called. "I've never seen a slug sit so still in the bull's-eye before."

"Concentration," Aldwyn said.

"Yours or his?" Brinn asked.

Aldwyn didn't answer.

"We all cheat here," Brinn said. "It's good to see you do it with such style, cat."

6

REVEALING GLASSES

Much was different about the New Palace of Bronzhaven. For starters it was hovering inside an enormous glass ball, and snow-flakes were falling all around it. Stranger still, desert stretched for miles outside the glass. Aldwyn was at the foot of a long staircase that rose halfway toward the bedroom window of the queen. Loranella herself stood at the balcony, her hair floating above her head as if she were underwater. Aldwyn bounded from step to step, desperately trying to reach her. She called out to him, but no sound left her lips. The words only *came out in letters that blew away like torn pages from a book.*

Aldwyn shot awake and discovered that he was lying under the oak tree in the heart of the forest that hid the Smuggler's Trail. Skylar and Gilbert were sitting beside him.

"You dozed off," Skylar said.

"We should go," Aldwyn said with extra urgency. The queen's plight was weighing heavily on him.

"What about lunch?" Gilbert asked.

"We don't have time for any more chores," Aldwyn replied.

"I worry that we haven't waited long enough for our pursuers to pass," Skylar said.

"That's a risk we'll have to take then," Aldwyn said.

The Three collected their scant belongings and returned to the trail.

"Gilbert, did they say you could take that?" Skylar asked.

Aldwyn turned to see that she was asking about the sluggot on Gilbert's shoulder.

"I didn't think they'd notice one little slug

gone," Gilbert said.

The group headed west on the Smuggler's Trail, toward Kailasa.

"Once we leave the woods, I'll cast another illusion," Skylar said. "It should only be a short distance across the plains to the Ebs."

"What are we going to be this time?" Gilbert asked, catching flies out of the air with his tongue. "Goat? Fox? A very small pony?" He lapped up another swarm of bugs.

"I was thinking pig," Skylar said, eyeing the mess of flies dripping from Gilbert's mouth.

"How'd you come up with that one?" Gilbert asked.

Normally Aldwyn would have gotten a good laugh over that, but right now he was too concerned to even smile.

"You okay, Aldwyn?" Skylar asked. "You haven't seemed yourself since you woke up."

"I had a dream," he said. "Queen Loranella was in it. I think she was calling for my help. But I couldn't get to her."

"We're doing everything we can," Skylar said.

"She was trying to tell me something, but

it only came out in letters, and they blew away before they turned into words."

"The Dreamworld often tries to send us messages," Skylar said. "And it's not always easy to understand them. There are no rules in the place where our mind travels while we're asleep."

"I hear something," Gilbert whispered to the others in a panic. "Quick, hide!"

"No need," Skylar replied calmly. "Remember what the bearded fairy said. The woods won't expose those who don't wish to be found."

She fluttered to the side of the road to avoid whatever was coming. Aldwyn and Gilbert joined her at the edge of the path. From there, Aldwyn watched as a band of warriors clad in black armor rushed toward them on horseback. It was the Nightfall Battalion. A large-eyed lemur rode atop the first horse. Aldwyn knew these creatures had the magical talent of seeing through solid objects, and it appeared this one had been enlisted as the Battalion's scout. The lemur turned its head from side to side, scanning the forest. Navid and Marati sat together on the second steed, while the rest of their troop followed behind.

The lemur held up its paws, slowing the group. The horses came to a halt just a few feet away from the familiars, but it was evident that their riders couldn't see them. The forest was doing its job.

"I spotted something through there," the lemur said, pointing past a cluster of dense trees. "A flash of blue."

Marati leaped down from her horse and went scurrying past the trio, into the woods. Aldwyn glanced over to the soldiers of the Nightfall Battalion, who were pulling noose sticks off their backs.

Marati returned with an oversized blue feather.

"It's too big to have fallen from Skylar's wing," she said.

"Looks like it came from a parrot or a pixie steed," Navid said from atop the horse.

"If they are hiding in here, they won't be able to stay forever," Marati said. The white-tailed mongoose practically brushed Aldwyn's paw as she walked past. "Let's keep moving."

The king cobra swung down his tail and gave Marati a boost back up into the saddle. Then the horses charged east, leaving the three animals behind in the magical cloak of the forest.

"I knew we should have waited a bit longer," Skylar said.

"Yes, but now we know the Nightfall Battalion is headed in the opposite direction of where we're going," Aldwyn said.

During the remainder of their trip along the Smuggler's Trail, the familiars didn't pass anyone else. Not that they were aware of, anyway.

Once out of the forest, Skylar and Gilbert were atop Aldwyn's back yet again, and this time they were traveling as a wandering mountain goat. The journey to the Ebs was not long, and was rather pleasant. Farmers tended to their spring harvests, plucking the winter pumpkins and frostcumbers from their branches. Tulips and crocuses were in bloom.

For several miles the Three walked alongside a cow and the dairyman who tended to her. Still in disguise, Skylar engaged in friendly conversation with the cow, and while much of the chitchat revolved around the best-tasting grass in the region, a few purposeful questions were able to make it clear that news of Loranella's near demise had yet to spread beyond the castle walls. Which meant the familiars' fugitive status was likely unknown as well.

After passing a trading village, Aldwyn came up over a small hill and the trio found themselves staring down at the Ebs, a thick band of blue hugged on either side by pebbly shores. The waters sparkled under the high sun.

"Hey, look at that inn," Gilbert said, pointing a suction-cupped finger toward a wooden building just off the main road. "Remind you of anything?"

Aldwyn couldn't help but smile.

"Looks just like Tammy's," he said. She was the orange-and-white house cat who had invited the familiars to stay in the innkeeper's barn during their first adventure across Vastia. "There's even a cat door out front."

Spice yachts and fishing boats glided upstream, propelled by phantom sails and silver oars. A golden bridge crossed the river, hovering above the waters with no wooden beams to support it.

"Do you think Banshee and Galleon had a hand in that?" Skylar asked.

"I don't know, but it looks like some wizard was definitely showing off," Gilbert replied.

"Then it probably *was* Galleon," Skylar said.

Bridges like these had been magically erected all over the land in place of the ones that had become river dragon fodder during the Uprising. And Banshee and Galleon, who stood with the circle of heroes, had been traveling across Vastia rebuilding the queendom to its former glory.

A pair of soldiers stood at security checkpoints on both sides of the bridge. Lines of humans and animals stretched down the road. The four guards held magnifying scopes up to their eyes, viewing each traveler as they passed.

"Those are revealing glasses," Skylar said. "They're able to expose any illusion by creating a yellow aura around it."

"Is there any way to counteract it?" Gilbert asked.

"Those devices are foolproof," Skylar said. "They were the creation of the great inventor Orachnis Protho, first used against the Phantasmanians, an evil sect of illusionists seeking to overthrow King Brannfalk. I never imagined one would be used against me."

"We'll have to find another way across," Gilbert said.

"Not necessarily," Aldwyn said. "Maybe instead of making the revealing glasses *not* work, we can cause them to work too well."

"I don't follow," Gilbert said.

"Skylar, would you be able to cast an illusion on everyone standing in that line?" Aldwyn asked.

"I don't know. I've never tried something of such magnitude before. Even if I could, I'm not sure how long I could hold it. Why?"

"If every man, woman, and animal trying

to cross that bridge appears as if they're hiding behind an illusion, those soldiers might start to think there's something wrong with the glasses."

"I do hold the Nearhurst record for most illusions conjured at one time," Skylar said. "It's worth a shot."

The blue jay lifted her wing and it began to tremble. Then right before Aldwyn's and Gilbert's eyes . . . nothing happened. Everyone standing in the line appeared just as they did before Skylar raised her wing.

"Not to be the slow frog here, but I'm still confused," Gilbert said. "I don't see any illusions at all."

"You're not supposed to," Skylar said. "I just conjured identical illusions of each person and animal in line. That way when they reach the bridge, the guards will see a yellow aura around them, but instead of suspecting that everyone here is trying to pull a fast one, they'll have no choice but to think that something is amiss with their revealing glasses."

"That's why I let you and Aldwyn come up with the plans," Gilbert said, still trying to catch up.

Ahead, the soldiers were starting to hold the

line, asking animals and humans to step aside. Confusion was setting in, followed by frustration. Angry travelers began to shout out.

"What's the problem?" someone yelled.

"Come on, let's keep it moving!" another hollered.

"Everyone, please, calm down," one of the guards called back. "We'll have this all sorted out soon."

But wiping down the lenses of their revealing glasses wasn't going to make this problem disappear.

Aldwyn, Skylar, and Gilbert, still appearing as a mountain goat, hastened to join the tail end of the line, and more people walked up behind them. The mob was growing more impatient by the minute. If Skylar was able to hold the illusion, their trick just might work. Finally the guards had no choice but to usher the crowd forward.

The familiars' mountain goat illusion blended in with the throng now crossing the bridge. Aldwyn, with Skylar and Gilbert on his back, had gotten about halfway to the west side of the bridge when he heard his blue jay companion groan uncomfortably.

"I can't maintain them any longer," she said.

"Just a little farther," Aldwyn encouraged.

"I'm sorry," Skylar replied.

Her wing slumped to her side, and suddenly they were exposed as the cat, frog, and bird that they were. Although the humans and animals crossing alongside them looked no different, the illusions Skylar had cast over them were gone as well.

"We need to get out of here," Aldwyn said. "Fast."

Aldwyn and Gilbert burst into a sprint, while Skylar flew above, but the quickened pace only brought more attention.

One of the guards standing at the eastern checkpoint spotted them.

"There they are," he shouted. "The fugitives!"

The other passersby on the bridge had no idea what was going on, but the four guards immediately pulled their weapons. From each side they began to close in. Aldwyn, Skylar, and Gilbert were trapped at the center.

"So you're absolutely sure you don't have any more of that Icari weed?" Aldwyn asked Skylar.

The guards were fast approaching, brandishing their swords.

Aldwyn thought for a moment about standing

his ground and putting up a fight, but the truth was, he was outnumbered. He glanced over the side of the bridge to the swift-moving channel below, looking for the river dragons. They made a habit of trolling these waters, giving locals and visitors alike a good reason not to swim across.

Then Aldwyn spied a fishing boat coming out from underneath the bridge, dragging its nets at the rear. It would be a long drop to the deck below, but if they were going to make the jump they would have to do it quick.

"Surrender now," one of the guards ordered. "We have been authorized to use force if needed."

"Skylar, get down to that boat," Aldwyn said. "Gilbert, follow me."

The tree frog followed his gaze to the passing vessel.

"Having wings makes it so easy," Gilbert croaked to Skylar.

The soldiers and their blades were nearly upon the familiars. But before they could strike, Aldwyn and Gilbert made a running leap over the side of the bridge. Aldwyn felt himself falling through the air, paws flailing, and it quickly became apparent that he had mistimed his jump. He and Gilbert weren't going to be landing on the boat. Instead they crashed into the water behind it.

The impact felt like a sledgehammer, knocking the wind from Aldwyn's lungs. He tried to suck in some air but instead swallowed a mouthful of river water. Then the tug of the current dragged Aldwyn under. He'd lost track of Gilbert, but all that was important was getting back to the surface. Only, he was sinking deeper.

Finally his paws hit something: rope. He'd caught hold of one of the boat's nets. With all his strength he pulled himself up rung by rung until he was above water once more. Gilbert already had his webbed hands wrapped around the tethered knot above him and Skylar was perched on the boat's railing, looking down at them in relief.

But they weren't home free yet. Arrows were raining down from the bridge, striking the water and the back of the fishing boat with their sharp tips. Aldwyn and Gilbert dodged the attack as they frantically climbed aboard the deck. A pointed bolt came flying at Gilbert, nearly impaling his neck but instead just clipping the now soaked cloth map slung over his shoulder.

Aldwyn glanced up at the four soldiers atop the bridge. One took a silver arrow from his quiver and placed it in his bow. But rather than firing it at the escaping familiars, he turned and shot it off into the northeast sky. It flew impossibly high into the clouds and disappeared.

"A messenger arrow," Skylar said. "The Nightfall Battalion will soon know which way we're headed."

"We've survived the Kailasa mountains once before," Aldwyn said. "I'm not sure those warriors can say the same thing."

Suddenly Aldwyn's nostrils began to tingle. He spun around and discovered a giant pile of river flounder. For the first time in two days, he smiled.

7

KETTLE FALLS

Aldwyn tore the last bits of tender meat from a tailbone before tossing the flounder into a growing heap of fish bones. Gilbert had eaten his fill, too, and the three familiars were taking full advantage of their midday respite, knowing they had a perilous climb ahead of them. There was only a small crew of fishermen aboard, but none of them had noticed the animals sitting in the back of the boat.

Gilbert hopped over to a pool of water that had collected by the storage chests. "Guys, over here," he said,

Aldwyn walked over to the tree frog's side and

saw that Gilbert was having a puddle viewing. Skylar flew above them for a look as well. There on the shimmering surface of the pool they could see Commander Warden addressing the head instructors inside one of the conference rooms at Turnbuckle Academy, identifiable from the giant symbol on the wall.

"No messenger arrows go in or out until those three animals are found," the commander said. "Jack, Marianne, and Dalton can know nothing of what's transpired. That way, if their familiars try to contact them, they won't know to warn them. It must remain business as usual."

"Surely the news will get out eventually," a woman with icy gray hair said.

"Not if I can help it, Instructor Snieg," Warden replied. "There will be queens' guardsmen keeping twenty-four-hour watch on the three young wizards. If that cat, bird, or frog comes within a mile of them, we'll know it."

The puddle clouded over, and Aldwyn, Skylar, and Gilbert turned to one another.

"I can't believe they don't know about the queen," Gilbert said. "Or us."

"It's better that way," Skylar replied. "The less they know, the less likely they'll put themselves in danger."

The boat was heading for an inlet where fish were practically leaping out of the water. Ahead, Aldwyn could see a path leading up the mountain.

"That should take us right to the Bridge of Betrayal," he said, remembering the route they had taken on their previous trip to the Alchemist.

"I fear the bridge we just crossed won't be the only one with guards on the lookout for us," Skylar replied. "Which means we'll need to avoid the Bridge of Betrayal and find another way around the Abyssmal Canyon."

"We were going to cross the Bridge of Betrayal?" Gilbert croaked. "I don't remember agreeing to that."

"No matter," Skylar said. "We won't be now."

"Gilbert, see if you can locavate a safe, alternate route to the Mountain Alchemist," Skylar said.

"I can try," Gilbert said.

Gilbert pulled the dripping map from his back. He unfolded it and carefully laid it flat on the deck floor in front of them. Gilbert then removed the orienteering stone from the pouch that dangled from the map's tie string. He set the stone down on the map and moved it to their approximate location.

"*Locavi instantanus.* Show us a safe, alternate route to the Mountain Alchemist." Gilbert lifted his webbed hands from the stone. Suddenly it began to quiver before darting west toward the Kailasa mountains. But the stone never got there. Instead, it made a 180-degree turn, zipping to the north. Then it started zigzagging all over the map, going every which direction. Finally it stopped back where it started.

Gilbert shook his head, disappointed.

"I guess I better stick to puddle viewing," he said. "At least I'm good at that."

Skylar used her wing to push Gilbert aside and stuck her beak close to the map, searching.

"There looks to be some kind of land bridge that crosses the Abyssmal Canyon," she said, gesturing to the map. "Beyond that point, it should be a straight climb to the Alchemist's cabin. Hopefully we can get there before nightfall."

"If there was another way up the mountain,

119

why would anyone take the Bridge of Betrayal?" Aldwyn asked.

"I guess we're about to find out," Skylar replied.

One of the crew members threw an anchor in the water and the boat drifted to a stop about twenty feet from the shore. Aldwyn and Gilbert jumped into the shallow inlet waters and paddled to dry land, navigating around schools of leaping trout. Aldwyn was surprised to find the water much warmer here than it was in the main part of the river. Perhaps it was from the sun shining brightly down on it. Skylar was already flapping her wings above the quiet beach.

"We can follow this stream uphill," the blue jay said.

Aldwyn looked and saw a trickling creek that led away from the inlet and up into the woods.

The Three began their walk. With no spy-balls, humans, or animals in sight, they decided it was safe to travel without hiding behind one of Skylar's illusions. They were able to move faster this way, without Aldwyn being slowed by Gilbert and Skylar riding him like a pony while he pretended to be a goat.

The path along the creek was unexpectedly lush, and the plant life was more reminiscent of a jungle than a hardwood forest. The higher they went, the more they were surrounded by palm trees and ferns.

"How odd," Skylar remarked. "Must be a fluke in the weather binding spells. It appears some kind of tropical front has permanently settled here."

Aldwyn felt it, too. His paws were beginning to sweat.

"It's rare that I get a chance to contradict you," Gilbert said. "But I think it's the water." The tree frog was standing knee deep at the edge of the stream. "I stopped to cool my feet, but this creek is warmer than the palace seaweed springs."

The quirks of Vastia's ecology were more inter-esting to Skylar than to Aldwyn, but now wasn't the time for the blue jay to stop for scientific study. So on they continued, each lost in thought. The climb became steeper, and the vegetation around the creek grew sparser. Aldwyn felt a gust of hot steam blow through his fur. He looked into the distance to find its source: a boiling waterfall.

"Kettle Falls," Skylar said. "I saw it on the map. Now we know how it got its name."

The waters bubbled furiously, like a pot of soup over a fire pit. A stone path snaked up the falls' neighboring hillside. Aldwyn could smell something odd ahead that reminded him of the fish and fowl shops in Bridgetower. His nostrils guided his attention to the nearby plunge pool, where boiled birds floated on the surface.

"Skylar," Aldwyn said, "whatever you do, don't look over there."

Naturally the first thing she did was look, and she flapped away in distress.

As the Three climbed the path, an occasional breeze would send droplets from the falls their way. Aldwyn's fur protected his skin from the hot splashes, but those that landed on his nose and ears caused him to twitch in pain.

Once they reached the top, they discovered a hillside covered in gaping holes.

"Something tells me those holes weren't made by prairie dogs," Aldwyn said.

Rivulets streamed out from each one, pooling in the falls.

"Does anyone else feel that?" Gilbert asked, his voice vibrating.

Aldwyn nodded, his paws trembling as the ground shook beneath them.

"Get back!" Skylar shouted.

Suddenly a superheated blast of water shot a hundred feet into the air from one of the holes. The geyser's spray came down like a deadly rain. Seconds later, it fell back through the aquavent, but not before frying everything around it, including an unlucky lizard who was scurrying past.

"Bridge of Betrayal, anyone?" Gilbert asked.

Aldwyn peered up the hill as more geysers exploded. They were about a hundred yards away from the edge of the Abyssmal Canyon and the thousand-foot drop between its walls. If the map was correct, there would be a land bridge that crossed it.

"A geological phenomenon like this should have some kind of pattern," Skylar said. "If we take a little time to study it, we'll have a fair shot at getting across."

"So, like I was saying, who's with me for the Bridge of Betrayal?" Gilbert asked again.

"Think about Queen Loranella, Gilbert," Aldwyn said. "She's trapped in the Wander right now, and in few days she'll be gone for good."

Gilbert slumped his shoulders. Skylar was already studying the maze of seemingly unpredictable bursts. She used her talon to scrawl notes in the mud beside them. Aldwyn didn't know where to start; to him, the geysers appeared as random as falling leaves.

While Skylar continued to look ahead, Aldwyn took a moment to look back, at all of Vastia down below. In the distance, beyond the mists of Kettle Falls and across the Ebs, he could see Bronzhaven and the New Palace standing majestically at the center of the city. To anyone glimpsing the magnificent tower from afar, it would be impossible to tell that the queen lay inside dying, and that only the strongest magical spells were keeping her from being pulled into the Tomorrowlife.

Aldwyn spied something else through the steam: figures approaching on horseback. He held his breath, waiting for the wind to blow a clear view of who it was behind them. Flashes of black armor. Slivers of the moon and stars. The

Nightfall Battalion had found them.

"Skylar, we need to go now," Aldwyn said.

"I'm not ready," the blue jay replied. "I've only calculated about half of the geysers' eruption patterns."

Aldwyn directed Skylar's beak down the hill, allowing her to see Navid, Marati, and the band of Vastian soldiers charging toward them.

"How did they find us?" Gilbert asked.

"They have every magical advantage the queendom has to offer," Aldwyn replied. "Olfax tracking snouts, swift-step spells."

Skylar was using every spare second to determine the frequency of the remaining geysers. But the Battalion was getting close enough for Aldwyn to hear the sound of horseshoes pounding against stone.

"Now, Skylar," Aldwyn said more urgently.

"Follow me," the blue jay replied.

Skylar took wing, flying diagonally across the hillside. She stopped short of one of the holes and held up a wing to warn Aldwyn and Gilbert. As if on cue, a geyser exploded from the opening. Once the water smashed down in front of them, Skylar continued her purposeful crossing.

Behind them, Navid and Marati dismounted their horses, as had the rest of their Battalion, all taking to foot. Without the strategy Skylar devised from watching the geysers' pattern, they stormed ahead, right into a burst of boiling water. The large-eyed lemur at the front of the group was lifted high in the air by the geyser before dropping hard to the ground in burning pain.

While one of the healing ravens who traveled with the Nightfall Battalion tended to the injured lemur, Navid and Marati led the others forward, not letting one fallen comrade slow their pursuit.

Skylar, Aldwyn, and Gilbert continued toward the land bridge, zigzagging to avoid the geyser blasts. To make matters worse, they had to dodge Navid's venom blasts and Marati's astral claws as well.

"Surrender before we're all killed," Marati shouted.

"We already told you, we can't do that," Aldwyn replied.

Another blast of steam nearly singed the white-tailed mongoose.

"The spell cast on that necklace, the necklace you gave her, was conjured from the components and hexes found in your rooms," Navid said. "And if there's one thing we've learned from hunting down criminals, it's that the innocent don't run."

"If we're trapped in some dungeon, there's no way for us to help save Queen Loranella," Aldwyn said.

There was no break in the chase up the hillside. Skylar directed Aldwyn and Gilbert through the columns of towering jets. She glanced back and saw Navid and Marati guiding their squadron directly into the path of a series of gaping holes.

"All of those geysers are about to explode at the same time," Skylar said to Aldwyn and Gilbert. "They'll be boiled alive."

Aldwyn knew that the Nightfall Battalion would stop at nothing to apprehend him and his companions. They'd lock them up in the depths of the New Palace and leave them to whatever fate the Council decided, whether it be life imprisonment or worse. But Navid and Marati were his friends, and the soldiers they led were good and honest, humans and animals just doing their jobs.

"Don't go any farther," Aldwyn shouted back. "Skylar discovered a pattern. You're heading straight into a death trap."

Marati seemed to consider the warning then stopped. "Everyone, fall back," she ordered. "Hurry."

The Nightfall Battalion began their retreat, and it was a good thing, too, because Skylar was right. The geysers exploded in unison, sending Navid, Marati, and their troop scrambling. It gave the familiars an opportunity to race ahead.

They reached the land bridge and realized that it wouldn't be an easy passage. Boiling water from the geysers on the other side of the canyon poured down its center, flowing into the stream that tumbled over the edge of the Kettle Falls. Aldwyn and Gilbert would have to tiptoe across the dry portion of the bridge to make it to the other side without cooking their paws and toes.

While Navid and Marati continued to pull back from the geysers, a pair of the human Battalion officers was bolder. They conjured force shields and charged forward. The spell protected them from most of the boiling waters splashing down, but some of the spray reached their skin, causing pink welts to form on contact.

"I told you to stand down," Marati called out.

But the men ignored her, racing for the land bridge with the hope of cutting off the familiars. Skylar was flying above as Aldwyn and Gilbert shuffled their way along the narrow strip of the bridge. It was only a matter of ten steps before one of the two soldiers was launched skyward, caught in a geyser burst. He let out a scream and fell to the ground with a crack.

The remaining officer reached the land bridge and pulled a noose stick from his waist. He sprinted along the edge of the bridge, avoiding the scalding water rushing past his feet. He extended the stick toward Gilbert and with a tug hooked the tree frog's hind leg. The soldier yanked him back, pulling Gilbert off the ground and perilously dangling him over the deep canyon below.

It took Aldwyn a moment to realize his companion was no longer hopping behind him. He didn't have time to act before Gilbert took charge. The tree frog reached for the sluggot still sitting on his shoulder. He squeezed it between his webbed fingers and flung it. The slimy critter flew through the air and smacked the soldier right between the eyes.

"Bull's-eye!" Gilbert exclaimed.

The soldier dropped the noose stick that had ensnared Gilbert, and Aldwyn used telekinesis to catch it just before his friend disappeared into the darkness. Aldwyn lifted the long wooden pole and circular net back onto land. Gilbert wriggled his way free as the soldier continued to stumble back, trying to fight off the slug, which was now attempting to crawl up his nose.

Gilbert caught up to Aldwyn and Skylar on the other side of the bridge.

"Nice throw," Aldwyn said.

"Nice catch," Gilbert replied.

This time, the familiars didn't bother to look back. Instead they looked through the clouds to the slope of the snow-covered mountains. Aldwyn could make out the three trident peaks of Kailasa, and he knew the Mountain Alchemist's cabin was not far now.

8

THE ALCHEMIST'S CABIN

"I know they say no two snowflakes look alike, but you could have fooled me," Gilbert said.

Thick blankets of white fell from the darkening night sky, coating everything on the mountainside in snow, including Aldwyn, Skylar, and Gilbert. With some steps, Aldwyn found himself neck deep in the chilling powder. Gilbert often disappeared altogether. Even Skylar was having trouble. She couldn't fly; her wings were too heavy with slush.

"We really need to tell the Alchemist to move

somewhere less out of the way," Gilbert said. "Maybe a beach house or a cozy little dwelling in Bronzhaven."

"Well, there's one plus to this storm," Skylar said. "It will cover our tracks and make it next to impossible for the Nightfall Battalion to follow us."

They climbed higher and arrived at the mountain spring. The trio had been here once before, on their first trek to the top of the mountain.

"Let's steer clear of that pool," Aldwyn said. "We don't need another close call with the Alchemist's pet pirahnadon."

They made sure to avoid the waters, and approached the next stretch of their climb with extra caution. The Mountain Alchemist had magically rigged the trail to his front door with booby traps, all in an effort to keep away trespassers. Somewhere along this stretch Aldwyn remembered a giant hand made of snow that attacked them with a barrage of icy snowballs. But as they proceeded ahead, nothing happened. Aldwyn certainly wasn't going to complain. The journey was difficult enough without one of the land's most powerful wizards playing games with them.

By the time Aldwyn, Skylar, and Gilbert stepped foot on the edge of the frozen lake, the snow had stopped falling.

"Oooh, a big one!" a deep voice grunted.

The familiars turned to see a giant cave troll crouched about halfway across the lake. He was clearly pleased with himself, admiring the foot-long fish he had just grabbed out of a hole he'd carved in the ice.

"That troll looks friendly enough," Gilbert said hopefully.

The gray, stony-skinned creature bit off the head of the fish and chewed noisily.

"He might want to work on his manners, though," Gilbert added.

"And that's saying something, coming from you," Aldwyn said.

"I'm surprised the Alchemist would allow a cave troll so close to his cabin," Skylar said.

"Unless it's not a real cave troll, but an illusionary one," Aldwyn said. "Another clever trick to scare off unwelcome visitors."

The troll chomped down the rest of the fish held in his stubby hand, accidentally biting into his own finger. The creature let out an angry growl, and he pounded a fist against the ice in frustration. The force of the blow sent a fissure along the surface of the lake, and shook Gilbert off his feet.

"Definitely *not* an illusion," Gilbert said, slipping as he tried to stand back up.

Grabbing another handful of fish from the hole, the cave troll rose from the ice and took long, lumbering steps back toward the mountain. The eight-foot-tall creature stomped right past the familiars. Clearly the troll was less than observant, and more focused on the bounty in hand than the one at his feet.

Aldwyn, Skylar, and Gilbert hurried across the lake. Once again, they were surprised to find their approach to the cabin so easy. On the Prophesized Three's previous journey they had to go under this lake, not across it. That was because of an impassable, invisible wall, one that now seemed to be dispelled. Perhaps the Alchemist had grown softer with age. Or maybe he'd seen that the familiars were coming, and decided to give them a clear path.

The trio passed the spot where the illusionary cabin once stood, and rounded a cluster of rocks before arriving at the Mountain Alchemist's cabin. It was just as Aldwyn remembered it, with a small porch out front and icicles dangling from the snow-covered roof.

They knocked several times, but no one answered.

"Hello?" Aldwyn called. "It's Aldwyn, Skylar, and Gilbert."

After waiting another moment, Aldwyn pushed the door open and the Three entered.

"Is anybody home?" Skylar asked.

They stepped into a sitting room that doubled as the kitchen, then moved past the fireplace. Only ash remained; whatever logs had been inside were burned completely. Cold porridge still sat in a pot, uneaten.

"Edan!" Gilbert shouted, hoping for a response from the Mountain Alchemist's time-stopping turtle.

But the eerie silence within only grew louder.

They headed down the hallway, stopping to peer inside the room where they had first met the

136

Alchemist. Just as before, the bookshelves were all empty, but now so was the chair. Even the solitary book that the Alchemist did own was gone.

Aldwyn, Skylar, and Gilbert hurried to the last room in the cabin, and there they found the entire alchemy studio destroyed. The apothecary cabinet had been turned on its side, all of its hundreds of tiny drawers littering the floor. Beakers were shattered. Gusts of wind blew through the broken windows. It was clear that the familiars were not going to find the Alchemist or Edan here.

"Someone came looking for something," Skylar said.

"The question is, what?" Aldwyn asked.

"Guys, look at this," Gilbert said.

They turned to see scuff marks leading out of the room, as if something had been dragged along the floor. The Three followed the trail of thin black lines left in the wood through the hall and up to a back door. They exited the cabin to find a large pile of snow with a glowing stone marker at its head, and although Aldwyn didn't want to believe what he was seeing, he knew what it was: a grave site. Someone had been buried here, and he feared it was the Alchemist.

"First Loranella, now this," Aldwyn said. "Something tells me it's no coincidence."

"We don't know that it's him for sure," Skylar replied.

Although Aldwyn was more than a little hesitant to do so, he used his telekinesis to move the snow enough to see the frozen face of the Alchemist. With an uneasy feeling in the pit of his stomach, he quickly covered it back up.

"Now what do we do?" he asked.

Gilbert had strayed away, unable to watch. But as he averted his eyes, he'd seen something else.

"Hey, I think this might be Edan's trail," the tree frog said.

Aldwyn and Skylar came over to take a look. Sure enough, there was a path leading away from the burial. While snow had fallen atop the prints, there was enough of a trace left to guess that they belonged to a tortoise.

"Let's see if we can't find him," Skylar said.

And as quickly as they had come to the Alchemist's cabin, they were leaving once more. Aldwyn was unsure if they'd be able to catch up to Edan before it started snowing in this region of the mountain, covering his tracks for good.

The familiars began heading downhill, moving as swiftly as they could. They hadn't traveled more than half a mile before coming upon Edan, trudging slowly through the snow. Lucky for them, he was a turtle, and speed was not on his side.

"Edan, we've just come from the cabin," Aldwyn said. "What happened?"

The tortoise seemed to look upon them with a heavy heart.

"There were too many for us to take," he said. "Even with our magic, the slow and the blind didn't stand much chance."

"Did you see who they were? Or what they had come for?" Skylar asked.

"They wore crimson hoods, and bracelets. Just like the one around your talon."

Edan gestured to Skylar's anklet.

"The Noctonati?" she asked.

"That's how it appeared," he answered. "Or people posing to be so. They were searching for the Alchemist's book. The one book he owned. The only copy in existence. Written by his grandfather

Parnabus McCallister. It was the thirteenth volume in his collection of divining spells. There are many secrets hidden within."

"Is there a spell that can cure someone of a parasitic poison?" Skylar asked.

"There is very little that the spells in that book are not capable of."

"Where were you going?" Gilbert asked.

"To Bronzhaven," Edan said. "To warn Queen Loranella that she may be next."

"You're a little late for that," Aldwyn said. "What made you think the queen needed to be warned?"

"It was my loyal's dying wish."

"But he didn't tell you why?" Skylar pressed.

"He didn't have a chance," Edan replied. "Has the queen already been attacked?"

"Yes," Aldwyn said. "There's been an assassination attempt. And the three of us have been framed. The best ravens and healers in the land are trying to bring her back, but she's stuck in the Wander. We have less than two days to save her."

"It is most unfortunate," Edan said, "for the Mountain Alchemist had an antidote for such a curse. And only two others did, as well. Kalstaff and Queen Loranella. It was knowledge the original Prophesized Three had obtained long ago from their own mentor, Somnibus Everwake. And they planned to one day pass it down to the next Prophesized Three."

"Then I'll contact them in the Tomorrowlife, just as I did the great architect Agorus," Skylar said.

"But it's too dangerous for you," Aldwyn said. "Last time you lost a feather. Who's to say what you'll lose this time?"

"That's a risk I'm willing to take. Now, if I'm to summon them forth, we'll need to find their gateway. A place of profound importance that will connect them to this world."

Edan gave a wrinkly smile.

"I know just where this place would be. Sixty years ago, after the defeat of Wyvern and Skull, Kalstaff, Loranella, and the Mountain Alchemist stood together on a cliff overlooking the Ebs. Zabulon, Paksahara, and I were at their sides. We were staring down upon the land we had saved from ruin when they said this was the spot they'd return to, if not in this life, then the next."

"Where exactly was this?" Skylar asked.

"The Turn," Edan replied.

The Turn was a bend in the river where cliffs had been raised by a powerful wizard to prevent a deadly flood. A wizard who just happened to be an animal.

"Before we go, could we trouble you for a time bubble?" Skylar asked. "We could certainly use the rest, and can hardly afford to waste the hours."

"Of course," Edan said. "Whatever I can do to help."

Edan lowered his head so that his chin touched the snow, and he shut his eyes. Suddenly a translucent shell formed around the four of them. It appeared as if time had stopped entirely outside the bubble, while inside, the world seemed to go on undisturbed. Stopping time was the tortoise's talent.

Skylar cast a flame fairy, causing the snow on the ground to melt and creating enough warmth so that they were comfortable. Gilbert was snoring within minutes. Aldwyn curled up to sleep. But Skylar was busy scratching her talon in the wet earth. She had written out the words again: "Spuowbip wjots sby udpjbm uosdwoyt."

Edan turned his head to see.

"What does it say?" he asked.

"I was hoping you could tell us," Skylar replied.

"I'm sorry," Edan said. "It's no language I've ever seen before. Are you sure you've transcribed it correctly?"

"I am," Skylar said.

She stared at the message for a few moments longer, then slowly closed her eyes.

Aldwyn lay there. There was so much to think about. So many puzzles that needed solving. His mind raced from one mystery to the next. But the answers would all have to wait.

He had fallen asleep.

Not a second had passed outside, but it felt to Aldwyn as if he'd been lost in slumber for the better part of a day. Once he and his companions agreed that they were all fully rested, Edan lifted his chin from the ground and the shell disappeared. The chill of the mountainside returned and final farewells would be quick.

"What will you do now?" Aldwyn asked Edan.

"I suppose I will continue on to Bronzhaven. I have been a stranger to the land for many years. I am interested to see how it's changed."

The familiars gave one last nod and began their journey to the Turn, leaving Edan inching his way down the gentle slope to the north.

As the dark of midnight approached, the moon was not even a sliver, making it difficult to see. Aldwyn was taking cautious steps forward, feeling for solid ground so he didn't fall off a cliff. The trip downhill was less tiring, but more strenuous on the knees. And unfortunately it was no faster than the trip up, especially given the low visibility.

"I had another dream about the queen," Aldwyn said. "This time I was standing on a rug in the middle of a field of dandelions and my paws started to sink into the fabric like it was quick-mud. I was being pulled in deeper and deeper, until I fell through a hole and landed in Queen Loranella's royal chamber. She was standing there about to tell me something but I woke up."

"I was dreaming, too," Gilbert said. "Well, it was more of a nightmare really. Anura and I were swimming in a pool of maggots as far as the eye could see."

Aldwyn shuddered. "That does sound terrifying."

"No, that was the good part. Then they all disappeared and we were sitting in an empty hole. Talk about a cruel joke." Gilbert had a faraway look in his eyes. "With Anura, I feel like it's the first time somebody's really gotten me. Everything in my life was finally starting to go so great. Now all of this. What's Anura going to think? What's my family going to think?"

"I don't want to go back to the way things were, either," Aldwyn said. "Before I met Jack and the two of you I was a nobody and an outcast. But no matter what happens, you're still you and I'm still me."

Their conversation was interrupted by the sound of hammering. They quietly followed it to a wall of ice. Through the darkness Aldwyn could make out a trio of howler monkeys chipping away at the ice with pickaxes. They held glowing torches, barely illuminating the night.

"What are howler monkeys doing this far from

the Forest Under the Trees?" Skylar whispered.

The monkeys broke through the frozen surface and one of them lowered a torch, bringing it close to the exposed object within. A mountain moose was revealed in the light, having been chilled solid for who knows how long. When the monkeys extracted it from the icy cocoon, they took knives to its hide and began to skin it.

"Ah," Skylar said. "They've come for its hide. This must be what they use to make their drums."

Aldwyn squinted and stared across the mountain slope. About fifty feet away, he saw stripes of red against the white snow. He looked closer and realized they were the wings of a giant moth, one born from the colossus sap at the tops of the great trees where the howler monkeys lived.

"Maybe we can ask to hitch a ride," Aldwyn said. "That moth could make the half day's journey by foot to the Turn in less than an hour."

"Probably best not to let anyone know where we're going," Skylar said.

"Then we won't ask," Aldwyn said.

Skylar and Gilbert both looked at him.

"I thought you left your criminal ways behind,"

Gilbert said. "That would be stealing."

"I prefer to think of it as borrowing," Aldwyn replied. "Besides, do we want to save the queen or not?"

As the howler monkeys continued to carve away at the mountain moose, Aldwyn, Skylar, and Gilbert began a quiet approach toward the moth. The insect was even larger than Aldwyn remembered. An elephant could comfortably stand on its back. The closer the familiars got, the more agitated the moth became, beating its wings nervously.

"We better do this quickly," Aldwyn said.

The creature snapped at them, but its leash was tied tightly to a rock, keeping it from snacking on cat, bird, and frog. The Three hurried atop the creature's back, and Aldwyn telekinetically unfastened the rope, freeing the moth.

"Gilbert, you're the only one with hands, so you need to take the reins," Aldwyn said.

The tree frog took hold of the long coil attached to the enormous insect's head.

"What, no complaints?" Aldwyn asked.

"I'll save my croaking until after Loranella is okay," Gilbert replied.

He snapped the reins, giving a tug on the moth's neck. It immediately started flapping. The commotion alerted the howler monkeys, who turned from the mountain moose and were soon running toward them.

"What are you doing?" one yelled. "Get off our moth!"

The insect was already airborne, leaving the monkeys jumping to catch its oversized legs.

"Wait!" a second howler screeched.

"We'll send the moth back as soon as we can," Aldwyn called down as the creature soared higher, taking to the clouds.

The familiars were now at the mercy of an erratic insect not known for its grace in the sky. But a bumpy flight was better than an all-night walk, so they braced themselves for the ride and watched the mountains and forest pass below them.

9

OLD FRIENDS

The moth flapped over the Ebs and approached a series of high cliffs on the eastern portion of the river. Farther south the familiars could see the intermittent bright flash of the Split River lighthouse. Each time it shined, the giant insect seemed to be drawn toward it, forcing Gilbert to pull hard on the reins to get the creature back on track. Skylar pointed a wing to the tallest cliff overlooking the Turn.

"There's the monument," she called out over the rush of wind. "Let's land."

Gilbert did what he could to steer the moth to the grassy peak. It hit the ground with a thud and Aldwyn and Gilbert were quick to jump off the creature's back. Skylar grabbed the reins in her talons and was trying to find somewhere to tie them down.

"Aldwyn, help me fasten these to that tree," she said.

Aldwyn gave a mental tug, and together the two were able to wrap the rope around a small sapling. With one last pull of his teeth, Aldwyn made sure the knot was as tight as possible.

Skylar flew toward the monument commemorating the Turn.

"If Edan is right, this is the best place to contact the Mountain Alchemist and Kalstaff," she said. "I'll just need to prepare a few compon—"

Just then she was interrupted by a ripping sound. They all spun around to see that the giant moth had torn the sapling right out from the ground and was now flapping off with the tree dangling from its neck. It was heading back for the Peaks of Kailasa in the distance.

"Next time, we'll have to find a bigger tree," Skylar said.

She dug into her satchel and removed a talonful of silver dust.

Aldwyn's attention had turned to the stone monument. Now that he was closer he could see that it was broken. The plaque once embedded in its surface had been ripped free and the gem that had been residing at its center was gone.

"That's strange," he said. "Who would want to deface something so sacred?"

"Probably the doing of Paksahara's minions during the Uprising," Skylar replied.

"I'm not so sure," Gilbert said. "Those cracks look fresh. If it had happened months ago, the rain would have washed away all the little pieces already."

"When did you become the detective?" Skylar asked.

"I've had my fair share of accidents," Gilbert replied. "I know my way around broken stuff."

Skylar closed her eyes and concentrated.

"Kalstaff, Yonatan, hear my call and speak once

more," Skylar chanted to the sky. She tossed the silver powder into the air and intoned, "*Mortis communicatum!*"

The familiars waited. Aldwyn recalled that the spell didn't take effect immediately when Agorus was summoned, either.

Suddenly a bluish mist began to appear. But as it materialized, the mist seemed to be getting sucked back into the hole that it was emerging from. The portal grew more solid, and Aldwyn could see two forms struggling to escape—the spirits of Kalstaff and the Mountain Alchemist. They were trying to break from the confines of the Tomorrowlife, but something was pulling them back.

"This isn't right," Skylar said. "A spell vacuum has been cast. Someone doesn't want us communicating with the dead."

Aldwyn watched as Kalstaff and the Alchemist trudged forward, fighting the invisible force that was trying to hold them back. While the vacuum might have been capable of preventing a lesser wizard from coming forth, it couldn't stop ones as powerful as these.

"Familiars, is that you?" Kalstaff asked, his voice trembling in the turbulent gusts.

"Yes," Skylar replied. "We've come to seek your help."

He was clearly having trouble hearing, as he spoke right over her.

"The children, are they safe? Did Queen Loranella hurt them?"

"They're okay," Aldwyn shouted back, loud enough to be heard over the spell vacuum. "And it wasn't the queen who captured them. It was Paksahara, posing as the queen."

"The trickery of a shapeshifter. I should have known."

Another strong pull from behind made Kalstaff stumble, but he stayed steady on his feet. The Alchemist was using his cane to push himself forward, coming up alongside Kalstaff.

"I've been murdered, haven't I?" he asked warily.

"That's right," Gilbert responded. "Just a few days ago."

"We have a question for you both," Skylar said. "An attempt was made on Loranella's life. She's been given a parasitic poison. Ravens and healers have been able to keep her in the Wander, but nothing's been able to heal her. We understand that the original Prophesized Three were told of a way to reverse such a curse."

"I know just the potion by heart," the Alchemist said. "Forty-three components are needed. First I will recite the essential liquids. Echo drool, water from the Wildecape Sea, dew drops—"

The force of the spell vacuum was getting louder. Now the familiars were struggling to hear. The Alchemist dug his cane into the ground, or at least tried to. But his desperate attempt to brace himself was futile. He was being tugged back.

"You'll never be able to say them all," Aldwyn said. "Were they ever recorded somewhere?"

"In one of my spell journals," Kalstaff replied. "I transcribed them myself. There's a secret room in the cellar at Stone Runlet."

"We know, we've been there," Skylar said. "How can we find the journal? There were hundreds of them."

"The inside page is labeled 'The Spells of Somnibus Everwake,'" Kalstaff said.

The power of the spell vacuum was becoming even stronger, and Aldwyn could see the two old wizards struggling mightily to stand firm. The Alchemist lost his footing for just a brief moment, but that's all it took for him to be sucked back into the Tomorrowlife once more.

Kalstaff continued to stand fast, refusing to give in to the force that had taken his ally.

"There's so much I want to know," Kalstaff said. "Please. Before I, too, am taken."

"The circle of heroes was reunited," Aldwyn said. "Human and animal now rule together."

"And the Prophesized Three?" Kalstaff asked.

Aldwyn, Skylar, and Gilbert didn't need to respond. All Kalstaff had to do was look at their faces and instantly he knew.

"Then Vastia is in good hands," the old wizard said.

"You were part of the Noctonati," Skylar said. "Do you know of any of its members who would want to betray the queendom?"

Kalstaff's resolve was weakening and the spell vacuum was overtaking him.

"There will always be enemies afoot in this land. Be the good that prevails."

And with that, Kalstaff was gone.

Skylar slumped down to the ground. Two of the blue jay's feathers, brittle from her tampering with the dead, fell to the dirt.

"Skylar, are you okay?" Aldwyn asked.

"I'm fine," she said.

"So I guess it's back to Stone Runlet," Gilbert said.

Skylar shook her head.

"No. Once I told the queen what we discovered in Kalstaff's cellar, she wanted all of his

157

possessions studied and archived. Commander Warden volunteered to house them in the library at Turnbuckle Academy."

All three familiars shared a moment of realization.

"You saw my puddle viewing," Gilbert said. "The queens' guardsmen have the grounds under twenty-four-hour surveillance. We may as well turn ourselves in."

"Warden said those guards would be keeping watch over our loyals," Aldwyn replied. "So we'll just have to avoid them."

"Sounds like a technicality to me," Gilbert said.

"It's the only way," Skylar said. "We'll just have to be extra careful."

"That moth sure would have come in handy for the trip," Gilbert said. "Without it, we'll be lucky to arrive there by midday."

"We better start moving," Skylar said. "We don't have any time to spare."

The Academy was located at the foot of the Yennep Mountains, to the north of the Chordata Plains, not far from Bronzhaven. Aldwyn didn't care that their journey was leading them in a circle;

only that a remedy for the queen was finally in reach.

The pungent odor of stinkweed permeated the dead forest. Centipedes and millipedes scurried over the mold- and fungus-covered ground. There were few places in Vastia that gave Aldwyn the creeps, but this was one of them.

"Did I ever tell you how the Weed Barrens came to be?" Skylar asked.

"No, but I have a feeling you're going to now," Gilbert said.

"This was once the most fertile land in the queendom. As green as the sky is blue. It was home to the elves, when elves were brave, before they became the scourge of the rivers. They cared for the plants, and got fruit and pure air to breathe in return. So abundant were the forest's offerings that others came to claim this wooded paradise as their own. But the elvin warriors would not be displaced. Until the Brotherhood of Hexes, a cult of curse-wielding warlocks who could twist the supernatural to their whim, overpowered them with deadly magic. Many of the elves were turned into centipedes and millipedes. The ones that escaped would go on to become the elvin pirates we know today. Unfortunately for the warlocks, once the elves were gone, the forest became this: the Weed Barrens."

Skylar perched herself on a nearby branch, one so dry that it almost snapped when she landed on it.

"Just give me a moment," she wheezed.

"I'd need to stop for a break, too, if I talked that much without taking a breath," Gilbert said.

Then without any further warning, Skylar collapsed onto the ground.

"Skylar!" Aldwyn called out in concern.

He ran up to his companion's side. Her eyes were rolling back in her head and her feathers appeared dimmer and without their usual sheen.

"I knew that spell wasn't safe," Aldwyn said.

"Well, it's too late now," Skylar replied. "The damaging effects of necromancy can be diminished by a simple potion. We just need to grind up some daffodil root."

"We'll gather some as soon as we're out of the Weed Barrens," Gilbert said.

"But that's not all," Skylar continued. "It needs

to be added to fresh milk."

"Fresh milk?" Gilbert asked. "Where are we supposed to find that?"

Skylar was too weak to stand on her own, so all she could do was lie there.

"I remember having a nice warm bowl of milk not too far from here," Aldwyn said. "Courtesy of our old friend Tammy. Gilbert, help Skylar onto my back."

The tree frog lifted Skylar and set her down on Aldwyn's fur.

"Hang on," Aldwyn said. "I'll do my best to make it a smooth trip."

Aldwyn and Gilbert pushed through the brambles. They steered clear of the roach-filled ravines and rotting carcasses of larger bugs that littered the ground. Bone vultures sat atop the high branches, stalking the barrens below for their next meal.

"The place really brings back warm and fuzzy memories," Gilbert said.

"Just keep moving," Aldwyn replied.

Skylar had gone so quiet, Aldwyn had to look over his shoulder to make sure she was still breathing. The blue jay seemed to have entered a feverish state.

"Jemma, Jemma," she repeated. "Don't go."

"Her sister," Gilbert said to Aldwyn.

Aldwyn wasn't the only one with a sister he was longing to be reunited with. Skylar had a deep love for her sister, too. But Jemma had passed on to the Tomorrowlife.

"Jemma, I'll bring you back," Skylar said. "Jemma . . ."

Her calls turned to murmurs as she became wearier.

Aldwyn and Gilbert exited the Weed Barrens and found themselves in the long, windswept plains that sloped down to the tip of the peninsula where the outpost town was located.

"I hate to be a worrywart, although being a frog, warts kind of come with the skin," Gilbert said. "But you ever think maybe Tammy and the innkeeper didn't survive Paksahara's Dead Army?"

"I hadn't," Aldwyn admitted.

Gilbert stopped briefly before a patch of still-sprouting daffodils. He dug them up with his hands and held them tight.

"Well, even if they did become zombie feed, there was a barn with cows and goats inside," Gilbert said. "Of course, there's no guarantee they would have survived, either."

Skylar was slipping further into delirium, now muttering words that didn't make any sense. She was burning up, too. Aldwyn could feel it through his fur.

He turned to Gilbert and said something the tree frog rarely heard.

"Gilbert, recite some of your poetry."

"What?" Gilbert asked.

"Your poetry. I think it might calm Skylar."

"She hates my poetry," Gilbert said.

"She only says that. Deep down, I know she'd find it comforting."

"Okay. Um. Let's see. Here's one I wrote about her." He cleared his throat. "Blue feather, wing, beak, each and every part unique, my best friend always."

Skylar groaned miserably.

"I'm sure that's just the fever," Aldwyn said.

The two continued on, past the dawn crickets crawling out from under the clover to play their morning song. The Three were getting closer now, and Aldwyn could see that the small outpost town still stood, looking no different from when they had visited here last.

Since Skylar would be unable to cast an illusion around the trio, the fugitive familiars would have to rely on sneakiness alone to get to the inn. Luckily that was Aldwyn's specialty long before he became one of the Prophesized Three.

Careful not to throw Skylar off his back, Aldwyn scooped up a pawful of the chirping crickets and put them in Skylar's satchel. He and Gilbert proceeded down a dirt road, stopping before crossing below a street lantern still lit from the night before. Across the way a cobbler was opening up his shop. Aldwyn telekinetically sent one of the crickets soaring past him, and as the man's attention was drawn away to the distraction, they raced ahead. Aldwyn pulled the same trick on a tanner and a group of tradesmen, allowing the familiars to safely reach the front of the small inn where Tammy lived.

Aldwyn poked his nose through the leather flap covering the pet-sized entrance cut into the front door. Tammy was curled up in front of a fire.

"Tammy," he whispered, hoping not to alert the innkeeper sitting behind the counter. "Tammy!"

She woke up and turned her head to look at him with her hazel eyes. Immediately they twinkled with recognition.

"Aldwyn?" she asked. "Is that you?"

"Yes," he replied.

She ran over to the flap and joined Aldwyn and Gilbert outside.

"I can't believe it," Tammy said. "I never thought I'd see you again." She glanced up to see Skylar shivering uncontrollably. "What's wrong with her?"

"We need some milk," Aldwyn said. "Quickly."

"Follow me," Tammy replied.

She led them around back to the barn, where most of the farm animals were still sleeping. A few chickens were already up pecking, but they seemed disinterested in the new guests. Aldwyn used his mind to drag a metal bucket beneath a nearby goat's udder, then telekinetically milked it. Once he'd gotten a cup's worth, Gilbert crushed the daffodil root in his hand before dropping it into the white liquid. Aldwyn lowered Skylar to the ground and used his paw to open her beak. Then with Gilbert's and Tammy's help, he tipped the bucket, allowing the milk potion to flow down Skylar's throat.

She coughed a bit, almost choking, before opening her eyes.

"Where am I?" she asked.

"We got you what you needed," Aldwyn said. "Shh. Close your eyes. Rest."

"So, Aldwyn the alley cat turned out to be Vastia's savior," Tammy said. "And to think, I knew you when."

"I thought about coming back to make sure you were safe," Aldwyn replied. "But everything was happening so fast. I never got the chance."

"I've always done okay taking care of myself. You shouldn't feel guilty. Besides, I'm glad you're here now."

She smiled, her tail curving toward Aldwyn.

"I'm going to leave the two of you alone," Gilbert said. "I'll just be over there by the pigs."

He hopped across the barn, giving Aldwyn and Tammy some privacy.

"Seems that it's safe to assume you haven't heard," Aldwyn said.

"Haven't heard what?"

"That we're wanted for the attempted murder of Queen Loranella. She's been poisoned."

Tammy gave Aldwyn a look.

"You sure do make a habit of getting yourself into trouble, don't you?"

"Not intentionally," Aldwyn replied. "But yes. I do."

"Any idea who might actually have done it?" Tammy asked.

"We haven't had much time to look into that," Aldwyn said. "We've been too busy searching for a way to save the queen. The palace healers said she would only last two to three days in the Wander. And it's already been a day and a half."

"Well, lay it out for me," Tammy said. "I'm pretty good at solving puzzles."

"It's quite simple, really. We gave the queen a necklace as a gift, and it poisoned her. The components for the hex were found spread out among our rooms. Things became a little more complicated when we discovered that the Mountain

Alchemist was dead, too. Who would want to kill the last two remaining members of the original Prophesized Three?"

"Maybe you're asking the wrong question," Tammy said. "Maybe what you should be asking is, *what* did Queen Loranella and the Mountain Alchemist have that someone else would want?"

It was a subtle shift in looking at the problem, but it immediately made Aldwyn think. What could they have had?

"Did anything go missing?" Tammy asked.

"Just a book from the Alchemist's cabin."

"And the queen?"

"Nothing. At least not that I know of."

"Then perhaps that's where the answer lies," Tammy said. "Told you I was good at this."

This time it was Aldwyn's turn to smile.

"See, I have talents," Tammy continued. "They might not be magical, but they could come in handy on an adventure."

"You're safer here," Aldwyn said. "Believe me, I'd love your company, but I couldn't live with myself if anything happened to you."

"Let me guess. When this is all over you'll come

back for me. I've heard that before."

"This time I will," Aldwyn assured her.

The two nuzzled ear to ear.

They stayed that way for a good while, until Skylar began flapping her wings.

"Good as new," she said, flying back up into the air.

Seeing her, Gilbert bounced back over.

"What's the fastest way across the Enaj?" Aldwyn asked Tammy.

"If you don't mind getting your paws wet, there's a shallow spot about a mile south. The current is slow and there are rocks to stop on for a rest. You should be able to swim to the other side without too much trouble."

"As long as it's not too much," Aldwyn replied. "A little I can handle."

He stared at Tammy. This was the second time he'd have to say good-bye to her like this.

"You think next time we can try and do this while you're not a wanted cat?" Tammy asked.

"Now what fun would that be?" Aldwyn replied.

The two rubbed whiskers and parted once

more. When the familiars hit the street, the sun had already risen and the outpost town was crowded with merchants.

"All right, Skylar, let's blend in," Gilbert said.

The blue jay raised her wing, and the three animals appeared to look just like one of the pot-bellied pigs from the barn. Except instead of a head it had a second rear end.

"Sorry, clearly I'm not back at full strength yet," Skylar said.

She lowered her wing and the illusion disappeared. They'd have to make a run for it as themselves. Luckily, no one gave them a second look as they headed for the river.

10

SAND AND STONE

A school of minnows was swimming circles around Aldwyn as he paddled across the relatively calm portion of the Enaj. Skylar was already sitting on the far bank, patiently waiting. And Gilbert had put his days as a waterlogged tadpole to good use, cruising to the other side.

There was a reason cats hated the water. It was cold and wet and made their fur itch. If Aldwyn could have gotten across faster he would have, but without flippers and fins, he was stuck flailing desperately. He took a break on one of the rocks, and Gilbert called out to him.

"Almost there, buddy. You're doing great."

"No I'm not. I feel like a dishrag with paws."

"Remember: paddle, paddle, splashy kicks," Gilbert said.

Aldwyn restrained a grimace, then noticed something.

"What happened to your locavating map?" he asked.

"I got it," Gilbert replied. "It's right here on my back."

"Actually it's not," Aldwyn said. "If it was, I wouldn't be asking."

Gilbert reached a webbed hand across his shoulder. He started to feel around in a panic. Then spun his head around.

"What? That's impossible. Where did it go?"

"You must have lost it in the river," Skylar said.

"Maybe I should start giving *you* advice on how to swim," Aldwyn said.

"Great." Gilbert sighed. "Not that my locavating was doing us much good anyway."

Aldwyn slid off the rock, back into the water, and kicked his way across the remainder of the channel until he reached his companions on dry land. He shook off the wetness and, with fur matted to his skin, looked about half his normal size.

"We'll cut through there," Skylar said, pointing to the long plains that stretched northeast toward the Yennep Mountains.

"And when we arrive at Turnbuckle Academy?" Gilbert asked. "Either of you given much thought to what we do then?"

"There are five hundred students and just as many familiars there," Skylar said. "Once we get inside those walls, we'll have to blend in and steer clear of Dalton, Marianne, and Jack. At least long enough so we can get to Kalstaff's journals."

"How will we make it through?" Gilbert asked.

"Illusion, disguise, and a lot of tiptoeing," Skylar replied.

The familiars left the banks of the Enaj and started heading inland. At the top of a hill they looked down on an enormous valley with thousands of stone chairs in rows of concentric circles, all surrounding a giant gravel pit. Grass had filled most of it in, but there were still crater-size indentations of black rock remaining. A ten-foot-tall sword was buried tip deep in the earth.

"Who would have been big enough to wield a sword like that?" Gilbert asked.

"Fjord Guards," Skylar replied. "This must have been one of Brannfalk's battle arenas. They were built all across Vastia to entertain the people during his reign. Warriors of all sizes competed within the rings, testing their skills for the amusement of the audience. Wizards and giants, dragons and elves. The victors would be rewarded with the adulation of the crowds. And the losers . . . well, they were given proper burials. Such sport remained popular throughout the land, until Queen Loranella outlawed it once she took rule."

Skylar's story left little doubt where the crater-size indentations had come from.

They continued their journey onward, passing the valley and approaching a long field of grasslands. They spied a traveling market that had been temporarily set up there. Even from this distance Aldwyn could see that driftfolk were selling their usual array of goods from the backs of their mule-drawn wagons. Smoke was rising up from a fire, and the smell of homemade stew was being carried on the morning breeze.

"What do you say we help ourselves to a little breakfast?" Aldwyn asked. "It's going to be a long trip to Turnbuckle."

Skylar and Gilbert agreed, and they headed straight for the makeshift bazaar. Aldwyn wasn't sure if others were just passing through like them, or if this was their destination, but people were in lines behind each wagon, waiting to trade for supplies.

Once they arrived, Aldwyn, Skylar, and Gilbert found a hiding spot near a wood fire set up beside the caravan. Aldwyn eyed an open sack of nuts and vegetables. A tattooed old man stoked the flames with a stick, his back turned to the stew ingredients. Aldwyn telekinetically dragged the bag toward them. The three animals dug in, noshing on cashews and celery. Aldwyn was about to bite down on a pawful of crushed corn when he heard a thunderous clopping coming from down the road. He spun around, expecting to see another driftfolk wagon approaching, but instead saw the horses of the Nightfall Battalion charging toward the caravan.

"Skylar, Gilbert—" he started to say, but they had already seen it, too.

"We'll never escape on foot," Gilbert said.

"And I'm too weak to cast and maintain an illusion," Skylar said.

Aldwyn glanced at one of the caravan's wagons. Two mules were standing up front, still harnessed to the covered cart.

"Gilbert, go talk to the mules," Aldwyn said. "Tell them they're going to need to move a lot faster than they're used to."

Gilbert hopped ahead.

Aldwyn looked to see that the Battalion was getting closer now. The lemur was once again on the horse up front, scanning the countryside for the familiars. Navid and Marati rode right behind.

Aldwyn moved to the back of the wagon and spotted a female merchant with bags under her eyes and stringy, unwashed hair. She was selling enchanted trinkets of questionable value and common household wares. He knew things would get awfully complicated if they stole the cart with her still inside. So he used his mind to send a half-dozen balls of alpaca yarn rolling from her display. The merchant huffed as she jumped down to the ground to go chasing after them.

Aldwyn leaped aboard the wagon, meeting Gilbert and Skylar inside. Gilbert gave a snap of the reins and the mules sprinted ahead. Customers scattered as the wagon was tugged forward. The haggard woman watched as her mobile storefront ran off without her.

"Liberty, King, get back here!" she shouted to the mules.

But Gilbert urged the mules forward, and they sped ahead.

The Nightfall Battalion rode through the driftfolk market, stopping to speak with the angry merchant. She was pointing at the runaway wagon.

"We're going to need a place to hide," Aldwyn said. "I don't think these mules are going to be fast enough."

"The Smuggler's Trail is too far from here," Skylar said.

As the Nightfall Battalion got closer, Aldwyn went on the defensive. He took inventory of the items filling the wagon, and assessed which ones might be helpful. A crate of crystal balls seemed like a good place to start. He mentally lifted them up and flung them. The glass balls hit the ground, rolling like oversized marbles into the path of the pursuing soldiers. The first horse's hoof came down awkwardly on top of one, and the horse tumbled nose first into the dirt, somersaulting forward and crushing the lemur beneath its weight. Navid and Marati steered their horse clear, but another behind couldn't avoid the fray, sending one of the human warriors to the ground as well.

The wagon rattled with such force, Aldwyn wondered if its wooden frame would crack. And even with two of its horses fallen, the Nightfall Battalion was hardly deterred, coming after them with more vigor than before.

"We're getting closer to the answer," Aldwyn called back to Navid and Marati. "You have to let us go and finish this. It's the only way Loranella will survive."

"Tell us what it is you think you know," Marati replied. "I promise you we'll follow up on any leads that might save the queen. But the three of you have to stop this before more people get hurt. Let the laws of the land, the laws that Loranella and Galatea put in place, work."

"Someone inside the palace set us up," Skylar said. "How can we be sure that anything that happens within those walls will be fair to us?"

There would be no simple compromise. The familiars weren't going to surrender, and the Nightfall Battalion wasn't going to let them go.

Aldwyn took mental grasp of a cauldron and chucked it out of the back of the wagon. Navid was prepared for the assault this time, and sent a blast of venom to intercept the heavy iron projectile flying their way. The cauldron was melted on contact, turning it into a pool of hot black ooze.

Marati countered with an attack of her own. A pair of astral claws reached out in the direction of Aldwyn, Skylar, and Gilbert. But the animals weren't the targets. The sharp blue claws slashed at one of the wheels on the cart, slicing back and forth at the spokes. The wheel splintered, breaking in half, causing the cart to wobble. Even the slightest shift in the mules' direction made the wagon teeter on the verge of collapse.

Marati's claws moved to the other back wheel, but before they could do the same damage, Aldwyn eyed a heavy burlap bag filled with flour. He used his teeth to tear it open and his mind to flip it over. A smokescreen of white powder blanketed the air, blinding Marati and forcing her to retract her claws.

A hot, dry breeze blew across the land, causing the flour to swallow up everything in its midst, including the mule-drawn wagon.

"I can't see anything!" Gilbert cried.

"Just keep 'em steady," Aldwyn said.

The winds picked up, sweeping the lingering powder out of their way. Visibility had returned and with it a most unpleasant sight: a giant lizard moving swiftly and silently across the ground. The creature seemed to be made entirely of sand, which constantly spilled from its back down to its legs. It licked up flecks of flour spread across the dirt with its long, leathery tongue.

"What is that thing?" Gilbert asked.

"A sandtaur," replied Skylar. "One of the wandering creatures from the Living Desert in the Beyond. The queen's border spells must have

180

weakened since she fell into the Wander."

The beast was on a rampage to confront the wagon head-on, and the spooked mules were panicking.

"Turn!" Skylar shouted.

"But not too fast," Aldwyn added.

Unfortunately Gilbert had already given the reins a sharp pull, and the mules were changing direction. They lurched to the left, putting all of the wagon's weight on the side where the rear wheel was missing. The pressure was too much, and the cart toppled, breaking into pieces. Aldwyn, Skylar, and Gilbert were tossed to the dusty ground.

The Nightfall Battalion was just coming out of the cloud of flour, unaware that they were riding directly into the sandtaur's path. The creature's leathery tongue lashed out and knocked one of the warriors from his horse. The warrior landed hard on the ground, not far from Aldwyn. The beast swiped a foot out at the horse with Navid and Marati atop it and wrapped its pebbly claws around Navid, clutching him. Marati leaped off the back of the horse and grabbed hold of Navid's tail. But rather than pulling her cohort free, she was left dangling in midair, too. A pair of aqua-blue phantom claws materialized before the sandtaur and began slashing at its leg. Grains of sand went flying in every direction, and the creature released its grip.

Navid and Marati went falling through the air. Just before they made impact with the rocky ground, Aldwyn telekinetically dragged a second burlap bag of flour from the mule cart and slid it right below them. The two made a safe landing, then rolled out of the way of the stomping sandtaur toward Aldwyn, Skylar, and Gilbert.

"We stand together for this fight alone," Marati said. "Afterward, we're taking you in." Her steely demeanor softened for a brief moment. "Thanks, by the way."

Aldwyn acknowledged her, but with the sandtaur bearing down on them again, there was little time for anything else.

The other members of the Nightfall Battalion had come up behind them.

"We all strike together," Marati ordered. "Except you, Navid. Wait for my signal."

The soldiers fired bolts from their wands in

unison, blowing holes through the creature's body.

"Fire at the head now!" Marati ordered Navid.

The king cobra sent a venom blast between the creature's eyes. The sandtaur's head crumbled and its body followed, crashing into a wave of sand that lapped up to Aldwyn's feet.

The familiars and Nightfall Battalion shared a collective look of relief, only to see particles of sand beginning to pool together and reassemble: the sandtaur wasn't defeated; it was re-forming! The head emerged first, snapping out and swallowing a Battalion soldier.

"Have any of you faced one of these beasts before?" Skylar asked Navid and Marati's warriors.

"Yes, once," an animal soldier replied. "I was worried that we were doomed, but then it started to rain and the sandtaur retreated."

Skylar's eyes lit up. She immediately reached her talons into her satchel and began rummaging around. The sandtaur, now fully formed, was thrashing its sandy claws out at anything within reach. Skylar flew over the creature and pulled out a talonful of bright yellow storm berries.

She threw them down at the beast, and quickly four gray storm clouds formed in the air. A tiny lightning bolt jumped from cloud to cloud, and then it started to rain. Heavy sheets poured down on the sandtaur's head, soaking the sand grains. The beast tried to escape, but it was already collapsing onto itself, its head melting into its torso, its torso into its legs. The swallowed Battalion soldier crawled out of the mess, gasping and panting.

Rain continued to fall, forming puddles in the sand.

"It's over," Marati said to Aldwyn, Skylar, and Gilbert. "Please don't make this any harder than it needs to be."

Skylar slipped a talon back into her satchel and this time pulled out some of her moist moss. She squeezed the component and incanted, "*Sutitauqa, sutitauqa!*"

Suddenly the pools of water beneath Navid, Marati, and their squadron turned to stone, cementing all their feet in place.

"Skylar, what have you done?" Navid asked.

"A reverse liquefying spell," she replied. "I'm sorry." Aldwyn and Gilbert turned to her, surprised. "Seems I've recovered quickly."

"You're just going to leave us?" Marati called. "What if another sandtaur attacks?"

"You've left us no choice," Skylar said. "Besides, you still have your swords, claws, and venom to defend yourselves."

Gilbert hopped over to one of the soldiers and pulled a rolled-up piece of parchment from his belt.

"My map," Gilbert said. "Thanks."

"I guess now we know how they found us," Aldwyn said.

Gilbert slung the map over his shoulder. Then he, Aldwyn, and Skylar hurried to one of the wagon mules and climbed atop its back.

"Liberty, let's go!" Gilbert shouted to the mule.

Aldwyn took one last look at the soldiers stuck in stone. Marati was already using her astral claws to try and cut herself free, and Navid was shooting venom blasts. But their attempts were yielding little success.

"We'll call for the spyballs," Navid said. "And we'll find you again."

"We know," Aldwyn said.

The mule charged ahead, up over a slope, and out of view from the Nightfall Battalion.

11

TORN

By mid-afternoon, Aldwyn, Skylar, and Gilbert arrived at the foot of the Yennep Mountains. From atop their mule, they looked out at a gathering of brick buildings that made up Turnbuckle Academy.

"I can't believe our loyals are here and we won't even be able to see them," Gilbert said.

"If they knew we were in trouble, they'd do anything to help us," Skylar replied. "Which is exactly why we can't tell them."

Aldwyn peered at a ring of a half-dozen walled-off training grounds surrounding the buildings, where students were participating in a variety of combat scenarios. In one, kids were navigating an ice forest while frost wolves hunted them. In another, young wizards crossed hills of black mondo grass, dodging flaming whirlwinds that spun in dizzying circles. In a third, spellcasters in training were storming a garden guarded by living topiaries wielding leafy swords and thorny bows.

Between the ring of training grounds and the brick buildings were practice fields where students were lined up in four-by-four groups. Each young wizard was performing synchronized wand exercises, led by a uniformed elder. Aldwyn's eyes scanned for any sign of Jack, Marianne, or Dalton, but they must have been elsewhere.

"Heading up the front path is probably out of the question," Skylar said, nodding to a walkway guarded by stone gargoyles lining each side. "Also, be sure to keep a lookout for any of the queens' guardsmen."

The familiars surveyed the grounds, and it appeared the only other way in was by cutting through one of the training grounds.

"What if we snuck across there?" Gilbert

suggested. The tree frog pointed to another walled-off area. It was an empty expanse of cobblestone. "If we hurry, perhaps no one will notice us."

Just then a lone sparrow flew past them toward the deserted square. The brown bird soared low to the ground. As it headed for the Turnbuckle Academy entrance, it was attacked by six vicious lizards, who'd been camouflaged by the cobblestones. Their razor-sharp teeth nearly chomped down on the bird, but the sparrow flapped into the air and got away. Unsatisfied, the lizards returned to their hidden positions, to await the next unsuspecting visitor.

"I'm open to other ideas, too," Gilbert said.

"I vote for the living topiaries," Aldwyn said, gesturing to the walled-off training ground with the garden. "Back at Black Ivy Manor, when Jack and I used to sneak out at night to explore, we'd tiptoe right past the ones guarding the estate. Sure, they never slept, but they had lousy vision. If we stick close to the outer hedge wall, we should be able to stay out of their sights."

Skylar and Gilbert nodded, and the Three dismounted the mule, who immediately charged off.

The familiars hurried down to the garden where the training exercise was under way. Aldwyn, Skylar, and Gilbert squeezed through the lowest branches. Once on the other side, they were thrust directly into the fray.

Two topiaries with branches shaped like crab claws went charging past them, nearly stepping on Gilbert in their pursuit of a young female wizard.

From the opposite direction, a rosebush trimmed in the likeness of a small troll ran by. The rose troll's arm thickened into a club spiked with thorns. It cornered a student, but the spell-caster in training had set a trap. Three more Turnbuckle pupils jumped out from a nearby hedge with wands at the ready.

"From green to brown, drop that spiked club to the ground!" one of the wizards incanted.

The rose troll's arm shriveled up, and the prickly club at the end snapped off, dropping to the grass.

"Go," Aldwyn shouted.

Aldwyn, Skylar, and Gilbert sprinted along the edge of the chaos. Despite their attempts to stay out of danger, the rose troll kept coming toward them.

Students were calling out to one another, trying to organize a plan of attack. The topiaries were far less strategic, but relentless. A Turnbuckle instructor calmly oversaw the exercise, offering tips to those engaged in the battle.

"Defenses up," she ordered a young wizard who looked overwhelmed. "Best to work together," she suggested to a pair of spellcasters fighting separately. "Stay away from spells with flames," she said to a pupil whose wand was sparking. "It may defeat the topiary, but you don't want to get yourself caught in a forest fire."

Aldwyn, Skylar, and Gilbert continued ahead.

"We need to find the library," Skylar said.

Aldwyn looked to the brick buildings. Each one had a gargoyle sitting atop its roof grasping something in its stone hand: a sword, a fork and knife, a scroll, and an hourglass. It seemed safe to assume that these objects represented what each building was used for.

"The library must be in the building with the scroll," Aldwyn said.

"Even I could have figured that out," Gilbert said.

The Three moved quickly the rest of the way. Students were busy coming and going through the front doors. Again, Aldwyn made sure their loyals weren't among them. With all the familiars walking and flying about, it was surprisingly easy for Aldwyn, Skylar, and Gilbert to slip inside undetected. Unlike the building's drab exterior, the entrance hall was vibrant with rich cherry-wood floors underfoot and floating chandeliers overhead.

"We're looking for a special room," Skylar said to Aldwyn and Gilbert. "One big enough to store all of Kalstaff's things."

The familiars traveled down the main hallway, peeking through every open door. Through the first, they saw young wizards and familiars inside a laboratory, dropping mud lizards into glass beakers.

"Now who here is willing to amputate a finger?" the instructor asked. "It's the only way to see if your regeneration potions actually worked."

Aldwyn and his companions couldn't stop, but they glanced inside the next classroom, where there were just a half-dozen spellcasters and a teacher. The students sat beside their own personal rectangular rugs, each with a swirling pattern spiraling on the surface.

"A dreaming rug is a mere portal to the Dreamworld," the teacher said. "It doesn't provide you with any protection or guarantees of coming back. Once you arrive on the other side, the rules of Vastia disappear. Even something as simple as a short stroll can prove a challenge for the most daring wizard."

As Aldwyn turned away from the door, three recognizable faces were coming their way. It was Jack, Marianne, and Dalton! They were busy chatting among themselves and hadn't yet spied the familiars.

"I had no idea there were so many kinds of gundabeasts," Jack said.

"Who knew some lived in trees?" Marianne asked.

"Skylar, Gilbert . . ." Aldwyn whispered urgently.

But it was clear they had spotted their loyals, too. All three darted for the nearest doorway and entered before they were exposed. Once Jack,

Marianne, and Dalton had passed, the familiars were about to return to the hall, when the classroom's instructor called out, "Ah, so our subject has arrived. I would have expected a lizard or mouse, but a tree frog will do."

Aldwyn, Skylar, and Gilbert slowly turned around. They were inside what looked like a science lab, filled with animal and human skeletons and anatomy charts. There were cages on the floor with barking lizards and mice that had grown dog fur.

"Up, up, here you go," the instructor said, ushering Gilbert to one of the experimentation tables.

Gilbert backed away, reluctant.

"Come on, Gilbert, play along," Skylar said under her breath. "Let's not call any undue attention to ourselves. That was a close enough call as it was."

The tree frog sighed and took his place before the class.

"All right, who's ready to try a full canine transformation spell?" the instructor asked. "We've succeeded in vocal metamorphosis and hair transfer. Anyone want to bring it all together?"

A shy girl who looked even younger than Jack stepped forward timidly.

"I think I can do it," she said.

"You?" another student asked incredulously. "You tried to turn a watermelon into a squash and blew it up!"

"I've been practicing," she replied.

"Since last night?" the student asked.

"Now, now," the instructor interrupted. "You can't learn if you don't try."

The girl walked up to Gilbert's side. Gilbert looked so nervous Aldwyn thought his friend might pass out.

"Think about the words you're going to speak before you utter them," the instructor said. "And remember to enunciate."

The young spellcaster cleared her throat.

"Maybe someone else can volunteer," Gilbert began to croak, but it was too late.

"Setting moon, snout of hog, turn this frog into a dog!" the girl incanted. She gave a little wave of her arm and shut her eyes.

Everyone waited. None more anxiously than Gilbert. But nothing happened.

"Well, good try," Gilbert said. "Guess you won't be needing me anymore."

Gilbert hopped down from the table, but all eyes in the room were staring at him.

"Uh, Gilbert," Aldwyn said. "You've got paws."

The tree frog looked down and saw that furry pads had formed where his webbed feet once were. And that wasn't all. His entire body grew bigger, and it was soon covered in a thick brown pelt. Whiskers popped out from his face, and a bushy tail sprouted from his behind. The next time he opened his mouth, all that came out was a bark.

"Wonderful," the instructor said. "You've done it."

He patted the young girl on the back. She sent a boastful smile in the direction of her disbelieving classmate then took her seat.

"If you wouldn't mind taking him down to the reversary, they'll change him back to his old self," the instructor said to Aldwyn and Skylar. "It's natural for him to be in a bit of shock."

Gilbert barked pitifully. He seemed to have an itch behind his ear, and as hard as he tried, his tongue wouldn't reach it. He attempted to lift a paw but was hopeless.

Aldwyn and Skylar quickly guided their unrecognizable companion out the door and the Three were again on the move.

"Obviously we can't take you to that reversary," Skylar said to Gilbert. "We can't risk running into our loyals again. But it should wear off eventually. I think."

Gilbert let out a disappointed groan.

"Besides, your little disguise might come in handy," Aldwyn said.

Gilbert was trying to say something, but his big lips and tongue didn't want to cooperate. All he managed to mutter was incomprehensible gibberish.

"It's probably better that we can't understand him," Aldwyn said to Skylar. "He doesn't seem very happy."

After peering inside another half-dozen rooms, they finally found the Academy's library. They entered and began wandering past long wooden tables filled with students engaging in quiet study.

"These are all common scrolls and tomes," Skylar said, gesturing to the walls. "The rare collections will be stored privately. Look for any doors to a back room."

They didn't have to search for long, though. The words "Special Archive" were etched into a glass door behind the librarian's desk. Beyond it, Aldwyn caught sight of a cavernous room housing artifacts and scroll tubes. He noticed the scuffed chain-mail robes and twin swords worn and wielded by Kalstaff in his younger years.

"Kalstaff's stuff," Aldwyn said. "It's really here."

Fortunately the librarian was assisting a student examining some globes well out of their view. Aldwyn, Skylar, and Gilbert hurried past the desk and sneaked into the archive. The first thing Aldwyn took note of was the temperature. It was colder here than in the library, which made sense, given the delicacy of all the papers stored within. To preserve them, a controlled climate would be ideal, and it seemed some kind of spell was providing that.

No one else was in the room save for the familiars, and besides the keepsakes from Kalstaff's cellar there were relics that once belonged to many of Vastia's other legendary wizards. One section was dedicated to the original familiar encyclopedias written by Phineus Pharkum. Another to Orachnis Protho's hand-drawn blueprints and prototypes for some of his earliest magical inventions.

Aldwyn's gaze returned to the robes and swords of their former mentor, alongside Kalstaff's other possessions of note. They were all labeled and mounted to allow for study. There was just one thing that Aldwyn noticed was missing, and he was not disappointed to see it absent: Yajmada's armor. His hair stood on end just thinking about the bone-hued helmet that had radiated pure evil.

Back when Aldwyn had first seen it in Kalstaff's cellar, the armor seemed to be possessed by a ghostly presence.

Skylar had found Kalstaff's journals and was already flipping them open in search of the page labeled "The Spells of Somnibus Everwake." Aldwyn and Gilbert ran over to help scan through the stack of journals, but Gilbert's newly sprouted dog paws clumsily fumbled through the pages, nearly tearing them clean off.

"Gilbert, maybe you should just guard the door," Skylar suggested.

He attempted to respond but slobbered instead.

Aldwyn lifted another pile of journals from a high shelf with his mind and stacked them up on the floor. He looked inside each one, hoping to find the antidote to the parasitic poison slowly drawing Queen Loranella closer to death.

After a couple of trying minutes that felt like hours, Aldwyn saw the words he was looking for.

"I found it," he called. "'The Spells of Somnibus Everwake.' This is it!"

Skylar flew over.

201

"There must be an index," she said.

She turned to the last pages and sought out the entry reading "Parasitic Poisons: Remedies, page 262."

Skylar's feathertips moved quickly, skipping back over large chunks of the book. Page 516 . . . 434 . . . 357 . . . 252 . . . She'd gone too far. The anticipation was taking its toll. Skylar slowed down: 260 . . . 263.

Wait. How was that possible? Aldwyn didn't understand. Skylar doubled back. Then turned the page again. In between, there were only jagged edges of torn paper. The evidence left little doubt. Page 262 was missing.

The spell they were looking for had been ripped out.

12

ANOTHER WAY

"It's gone," Aldwyn said.

"I can see that," Skylar replied.

Gilbert chimed in with an angry growl.

"Whoever's behind all this has beaten us here, too," Aldwyn said. "Now we'll have no way to pull Loranella from the Wander."

"This was the last remaining record of an antidote," Skylar said. "And the only person still breathing who can tell us how to re-create it is the very victim of the poison itself."

"Remember those dreams I've been telling you about?" Aldwyn said. "The ones with Queen Loranella. I keep thinking there was a message she was trying to send me. But I'm still not sure what it was."

All of a sudden Gilbert began barking. He trotted over to them, tail wagging.

"What is it, Gilbert?" Skylar asked.

He tried again to speak but still couldn't form the words. Frustrated, he started to pantomime instead, lying down on the floor and snoring.

"Gilbert, we're all tired," Skylar said. "But now isn't the time for a nap."

Gilbert shook his head and made another attempt. This time he walked over to one of the library's small rugs and began scratching at it.

"I don't understand," Aldwyn said. "Are you digging for something?"

Gilbert smacked a paw against his head and gave up.

"I just wish we could wake Loranella up for a minute, or she could talk in her sleep," Aldwyn said. "Something so she could tell us how to fix this."

Skylar clapped her wings together.

"That's it," she said. "I think there's a way she *can* talk to us in her sleep. In the Dreamworld!

We can use those dreaming rugs we saw in the classroom and go to her."

"Skylar, you're a genius," Aldwyn exclaimed.

Gilbert was frantically looking from Aldwyn to Skylar, then to the small rug he had been scratching. Then he pantomimed sleep and snoring just as he had done moments before.

"For goodness' sake, Gilbert," Skylar said, "if you're really that exhausted, just lie down for a minute. You don't have to make such a big fuss about it."

Gilbert drooped his head back into his paws.

"Could that really work?" Aldwyn asked Skylar.

"It could work, but it won't be easy. And to be perfectly honest, the Dreamworld's not a place I know very much about. Only that it's more dangerous than anywhere we've been before." Skylar and Aldwyn shared a look of resolve. "We'll have to get a dreaming rug of our own, and learn how to use it."

"How are we going to do that?" Aldwyn asked.

"There must be some kind of manual or guidebook in the library," Skylar said. "Although I'm not really certain we have time to look for it."

"I have another idea," Aldwyn said. "But you're not going to like it."

"I'm not liking a whole lot about any of this," Skylar replied.

The Three headed back for the glass door and made sure no one was in sight before sneaking out. They raced through the library and quickly returned to the Academy's corridors. After making their way back down the hall, they stopped in front of the smaller classroom where the teacher had been instructing her students about the Dreamworld. Only five young wizards were inside now. Some had cuts and bruises. One had claw marks across his forehead, with the blood still fresh and dripping, but instead of getting help they were staring at their missing classmate's dreaming rug.

"Another minute," the teacher said. "Then I'll go in myself."

The pattern at the center of one of the rectangular rugs started swirling and a hand reached out. The teacher quickly grabbed the hand and pulled the girl from the rug.

"I took just one step off the path you mapped

out for me," the student muttered, nearly delirious.

"Consider yourself lucky you returned at all," the teacher said. "Embeth, be a dear and take Daphne down to the infirmary. The rest of you are dismissed."

Aldwyn, Skylar, and Gilbert ducked around the corner and waited for the students to depart before they slipped through the open door. The teacher was wiping the day's lesson plan from a slate.

"Familiars," she said upon spotting them, "where are your loyals?"

Aldwyn telekinetically slammed the door shut, then turned to the chair at the teacher's desk. He dragged it up behind her and mentally pushed her into it.

"What is the meaning of this?" she asked.

"I'm very sorry," Aldwyn replied. "But this is a matter of life or death for Queen Loranella. We can't even be certain she'll make it through the night."

He tore a curtain from the window and used it to telekinetically bind the teacher's wrists and ankles to the chair.

"*This* was your idea?" Skylar asked Aldwyn. "Kidnapping the instructor?"

"I told you you wouldn't like it," Aldwyn said.

The teacher struggled but couldn't wriggle free or reach the wand sitting atop her desk.

"We don't want to hurt you," Aldwyn assured her. "We just need your help."

"Now I recognize you," she said. "You're Aldwyn and Skylar." Then her attention turned to Gilbert. "Actually, I'm not sure who you are."

Gilbert gave a frustrated yip.

"My next class starts in a few minutes," the teacher said. "They'll catch you."

"Then we'd better be quick," Skylar said. "We have to speak to Loranella, and we believe she can be contacted in the Dreamworld. Tell us everything we need to know. How to get in, how to get out . . . and how to avoid the dangers once we're inside."

"It takes years of practice to navigate such a world," the teacher replied. "The place our minds go when we sleep is unpredictable and ever changing. A locale you visit one minute might not be there the next. And the pathways between them never lead you in straight lines. They go every which way."

"Why don't you start with the basics?" Aldwyn asked. "How do those dreaming rugs work?"

"All you need to do is lie down on one and close your eyes, and it will transport you to the land of dreams. But never forget, a physical visit is not the same as one you make while sleeping. Unlike a trip taken by your subconscious, traveling through a dreaming rug leaves you vulnerable to all the hazards the world has to offer."

"And once we've found the queen and gotten the answers we need," Skylar said, "how do we get out?"

"You must take a thread from your rug and pull it behind you," the teacher said. "You can never lose it, though, for it will be the only way to find your way back."

The sound of a bell clanged through the halls.

"My students will be arriving for class soon," the teacher warned.

"When we come through the other side, how do we locate the queen?" Skylar asked.

"If in this world she's at rest in the New Palace of Bronzhaven, then in that one you should find her waiting in the Palace of Dreams," the teacher said. "But even I have never made a journey that far."

"Then what do you recommend we do?" Aldwyn asked.

"Find a remwalker to guide you. You'll recognize them by their bright red eyes, for they never sleep."

Suddenly the door handle began to rattle.

"Help me!" the teacher cried. "I've been taken—"

Aldwyn telekinetically lifted the cloth she'd been using to wipe down the slate and flung it across the room and into her mouth, gagging her.

"Again, my apologies," he said.

Skylar was already rolling up a dreaming rug.

"What are you doing?" Aldwyn asked.

"We can't travel through here," Skylar replied. "Remember, you come out the same place you go in. No doubt they'd be waiting for us."

"Good point," Aldwyn said.

"Now come on, help me get this up on Gilbert's back," Skylar said.

Aldwyn mentally lifted the rug into the air and set the bundle atop Gilbert.

"See, I told you this dog thing would come in handy," Aldwyn said.

The attempts to open the door from the hall were growing more urgent and students' voices could be heard. "Instructor Weaver, is everything okay in there?"

The cloth in her mouth prevented her from calling out.

Skylar turned to her companions. "Once Aldwyn opens that door, we make a run for it. Gilbert, whatever you do, don't let that rug fall off your back."

Gilbert let out a bark to indicate he understood.

"All right, here we go," Aldwyn said.

He used his mind to unbolt the lock, and the door swung open. Immediately students came rushing in to find their teacher bound and gagged, but Aldwyn, Skylar, and Gilbert were sprinting through their legs for the hall. Gilbert was moving so fast it was hard to keep up.

The familiars never looked back, charging down toward the exit. A student shouted out from the dreaming rug classroom. "We've got intruders!"

Aldwyn, Skylar, and Gilbert burst out the front doors of the brick building. A pack of Turnbuckle students and instructors were racing toward the growing commotion.

"Can't you two go any faster?" Gilbert called out.

Aldwyn and Skylar shared a look. Gilbert's face had shed its shaggy beard and his mouth had returned to the smooth amphibious lips of a tree frog.

"Hey, I can talk again," Gilbert said.

Aldwyn glanced ahead and saw Commander Warden at the front of the group.

"Stop those familiars," he ordered. "They're wanted for treason against the queen."

Aldwyn, Skylar, and Gilbert were running for the ring of walled-off training grounds. "Oh, boy, there goes my tail," Gilbert said.

Aldwyn looked over to see that the furry dog tail had shrunk back into Gilbert's butt, and the tree frog was beginning to return to his normal size.

The three animals stayed close as bolts of magic went whizzing by them. A young wizard made a diving leap, reaching out to grab Aldwyn. But just as his fingers took hold of the cat's tail, he was shot back by a wand blast.

Aldwyn turned to see Jack, with his wand outstretched. Dalton and Marianne were at his side.

"Aldwyn, what are you doing here?" Jack asked. "Does this have something to do with Yeardley?"

"No, the search for my sister got slightly sidetracked," Aldwyn replied.

"What's Commander Warden talking about?" Jack continued. "What treason against the queen?"

"We've been framed," Aldwyn replied. "They think we tried to kill Loranella. And the only way to clear our names is by saving her."

"It's best if the three of you stay out of this," Skylar said. "There's no point in giving them any reason to think you're involved, too."

"We're not leaving, if that's what you're suggesting," Dalton replied. "You've never turned your backs on us when we've been in trouble."

The familiars continued their dash, with their loyals right behind them. But now it wasn't just Warden and the Turnbuckle wizards giving chase. Two of the queens' guardsmen, no doubt the ones assigned to keep watch over Jack, Marianne, and Dalton, were in pursuit, too.

"Guys, a little help here," Gilbert croaked.

Aldwyn and Skylar saw that their companion had returned to his former state, save for two floppy dog ears. The rug that Gilbert had been carrying so easily just moments earlier was now far too heavy for him to hold.

"Gilbert, what happened to you?" Marianne asked.

"Long story," the tree frog said in a muffled voice from beneath the rug.

Marianne lifted it off Gilbert's back and he was free to hop once more.

"How do we get out of here?" Aldwyn asked.

"Your only choice is to cut through the training grounds," Dalton replied.

This time they wouldn't have the luxury of picking which one. It would have to be the walled-off area with the vicious camouflage lizards, because it was closest, and Warden, the Turnbuckle wizards, and the queens' guardsmen were closing in.

"We'll hold them back," Jack said.

"We can't let you do that," Skylar replied.

"Go," Dalton insisted.

Skylar took one end of the rug in her talons, and Aldwyn the other in his mouth.

Jack, Marianne, and Dalton stood side by side, raising their palms into the air and conjuring a large, ghostly hand between them and the rapidly approaching mob. The force push sent the first wave of wizards tumbling backward. It gave the familiars enough time to squeeze past the outer hedge lining the training area. Skylar and Aldwyn struggled to pull the rug as well. It got stuck in the branches, taking all of Aldwyn's clawing and scraping to get it through.

Skylar lifted her wing, casting an illusion. It was of a sparrow, just like the one that had attracted the camouflaged lizards before. The ferocious creatures made themselves seen, attacking the nonexistent bird. With Skylar's distraction keeping the lizards away, the familiars resumed their escape, dreaming rug in tow. Unfortunately any hope the familiars had of making it through the other side were squashed for good when the opposite wall opened up as well to let another group of spellcasters charge toward them. There was no direction where danger wasn't near. They were trapped.

Instructor Snieg, the icy-gray-haired woman from Gilbert's puddle viewing, approached.

"Noble as you claim your intentions to be, Galatea has requested your capture and immediate return to Bronzhaven," she said. "We'd much rather take you in alive than be forced to scrape up your remains once the razoracs are finished with you."

Aldwyn looked at the giant, toothy lizards crawling toward them.

"Lay down the rug," Aldwyn whispered to his companions.

"Here?" Skylar asked. "What if those creatures destroy it? There will be no way to get out."

Aldwyn glanced through a narrow slit in the branches of the outer hedge to see that their loyals and the ethereal hand were still pushing back the relentless assault.

"And no way for Warden or the others to come in after us," Aldwyn replied. "Assuming Jack, Marianne, and Dalton don't keep them at bay forever."

"Then we'll be trapped in the Dreamworld," Skylar said.

"Not if we find another exit," Aldwyn countered.

"But what if there isn't one?" Skylar asked.

Gilbert was unrolling the rug so it was flat on the cobblestones.

"Don't be fools," Snieg shouted. "Whatever fate the queendom has in store for you surely will be better than the path you're about to take."

Aldwyn, Skylar, and Gilbert were about to find out.

"Everyone, close your eyes," Skylar said.

The Three lay down on the swirling pattern at the rug's center. As his eyes shut, Aldwyn felt the ground beneath him suddenly give way, and he was falling. Even though he was tumbling through some kind of space between, he opened his eyes to see the razoracs shredding the rug to nothing but tiny bits of string.

When Aldwyn emerged from the churning darkness, his feet were touching down on what looked like cobblestones but were actually the shells of a thousand tortoises standing side by side. Skylar and Gilbert landed next to him.

Aldwyn did a full circle, taking in the Dreamworld for the first time. The Three had arrived just outside an alternate version of Turnbuckle Academy. Here, each of the gray buildings stood six feet above the ground, each atop the four legs of a horse. The buildings trotted about, as if grazing in a field.

Aldwyn watched a flock of bats fly overhead. The sun, hanging low in the sky, lashed out a fiery tongue, swallowing up three of them.

"Maybe Snieg was right," Aldwyn said.

"Well, it's too late now," Skylar replied. "We better start looking for one of those remwalkers."

"I feel like I'm dreaming," Gilbert said. "Are you sure we're awake?"

Skylar reached out her talon and pinched Gilbert hard on the arm.

"Owww," the tree frog cried.

"Yep, I'm sure," Skylar said.

The Three set off to the north, walking across the backs of the tortoiseshells. There was no guarantee that Queen Loranella was even still alive. But if she was holding on, their only hope now was to find her in the Palace of Dreams.

13

REMWALKER

"It's certainly not what I was expecting," Skylar said.

"Which part?" Gilbert asked. "The polished silver mountains or lava waterfalls?"

"Both," Skylar replied. "All of it. Somehow I never imagined it to be this big. I must not have traveled very far in my dreams."

The familiars had been walking for only a quarter of a mile, but they'd passed through a dizzying number of different locations, each one blending into the next with no warning. They had avoided danger thus far, and hadn't seen any other people or animals.

"When I was a tadpole, I used to have this recurring dream," Gilbert said. "I was in the swamp, but everything around me was enormous. The reeds were as tall as trees. Lily pads looked like giant islands. Even the flies were as massive as dragons."

"Sounds like the canopy we visited in the Forest Under the Trees," Aldwyn said.

"No, it felt different," Gilbert said. "It wasn't so much that everything else was big. It was that I was small."

"You've come a long way since then," Skylar said. "You've made your family proud."

Aldwyn, Skylar, and Gilbert continued to head north toward the palace, or at least what they thought was north. Everything was warped and twisted, throwing their sense of direction completely off. Even the mountains and trees seemed to have rotated.

"How are we supposed to get to the palace if we keep going in circles?" Skylar asked.

"We'd better find that remwalker," Aldwyn said.

"Where?" Gilbert asked. "We haven't seen

another soul since we got here."

"What about up there?" Aldwyn replied.

He pointed to a city in the clouds, actual brick buildings standing among puffs of white suspended in the air, high above the forest in the distance. They could see a heavy rain falling.

"It looks like as good a place to start as any," Skylar said.

They continued forward, only to come upon a river rushing across their path without warning. Ten feet wide, it was filled with teeth. Incisors, cuspids, and molars clattered past, making a noise that reminded Aldwyn of the sound his own teeth would make after taking shelter from a cold rain.

"I've dreamed of losing teeth before," Aldwyn said.

"How do you suggest we get across?" Gilbert asked. "I don't think we can walk or swim through that."

Just then, they saw an older woman wash by in the current. She was struggling to keep her head above the piles of teeth.

"Help me!" she called out. "Please, somebody!"

"What should we do?" Gilbert asked.

"She'll be fine," Skylar replied. "She's only dreaming. Nothing can happen to her."

Aldwyn knew Skylar was right, but he couldn't just stand by and watch someone suffer. He eyed a nearby tree branch and telekinetically bent it to her. She reached out and grabbed it.

As she dragged herself to shore, the old woman disappeared.

"She must have woken up," Skylar said.

"Maybe if we wait here long enough, the river will clear," Gilbert said.

The Three sat on the bank waiting patiently, watching as other dreamers were swept along in the flow. Aldwyn saved another one or two, but seeing as how they vanished once he was finished, it didn't seem necessary. For them, none of this was real. They'd stop dreaming, their eyes would open, and they'd be safe beneath the covers of their beds.

The torrent of teeth didn't seem to be letting up, and soon, the familiars spotted its biggest victim yet: a fifteen-foot-tall Fjord Guard. It hadn't occurred to Aldwyn until then that, large or small, everyone who sleeps dreams. The giant was so large he took up nearly the entire width of the river. And that gave Aldwyn an idea.

"Gilbert, when that Fjord Guard goes by, jump for his arm," Aldwyn said. "Try to use him as a bridge to the other side."

There wasn't a whole lot of time to discuss it. As soon as the giant was within reach, Aldwyn and Gilbert took a running jump and landed on his shoulder. Skylar, as usual, had the advantage of flying above.

"This isn't a part of the dream I've ever had before," the Fjord Guard shouted as the cat and tree frog bounded across his beard.

The giant was beginning to sink deeper into the teeth, making Aldwyn and Gilbert's race to shore even more urgent. They made a final sprint down the Fjord Guard's other arm and leaped for the far bank. Skylar was there waiting for them. The river of teeth continued to rattle and flow, but the path ahead was clear.

As they got closer to the forest, Aldwyn could see that what he'd first thought to be heavy rain was really people and animals falling from the sky.

A man dressed in the ragged pants and tunic of a farmhand tumbled through the air, letting out a frightened scream. He hurtled toward the ground, but before he made contact he disappeared.

Dozens of others were experiencing the same thing. Falling horses whinnying in terror. Children covering their eyes in fear. Yet none of them hit the earth. They all vanished just in time.

"Another common dream," Aldwyn said. "Falling."

"I've had my share of those," Gilbert added.

"Not me," Skylar said. "Must not be a bird thing."

225

Aldwyn turned his attention away from the plummeting dreamers to the forest itself. To his surprise—although nothing in this world really should have come as a surprise anymore—the tree trunks were leafy ladders that stretched to the clouds.

"If we're going to find what's up there, I suppose we should start climbing," Aldwyn said, stopping before one of the ladders.

"And if it breaks and we fall?" Gilbert asked. "We don't get to disappear before meeting our deaths."

Aldwyn put his paws on the ladder and began to ascend it rung by rung. It wobbled and swayed, but Gilbert followed, and Skylar flew at their sides. The Three continued higher and higher.

When Aldwyn reached the lowest layer of the clouds, it felt like he was entering a thick fog. He wasn't able to see much past the tips of his own whiskers. Soon a commotion could be heard above, the sound of footsteps accompanied by the din of a crowd chattering.

After another twenty rungs, Aldwyn emerged into a courtyard glowing in the evening sunset.

Gilbert and Skylar came up behind him and they found themselves among a rush of humans, animals, and creatures. Some walked around confused by the disorienting surroundings. Others went about their business as if they lived there. Aldwyn was paying particularly close attention to the eyes of the passersby, looking for the red tint that the Turnbuckle instructor said would expose a remwalker. No one matched the description yet.

"Apparently these remwalkers don't want to be found," Aldwyn said, frustrated.

"This way," Skylar said.

She flew from the courtyard toward a main road lined with vendors selling trinkets and inventions advanced beyond anything Aldwyn had ever seen conjured by Vastian wizards or black marketeers. Great spellcasters often said that moments of profound insight about conjuring new magic struck them in their sleep. Perhaps, Aldwyn thought, Kalstaff or the original members of the First Phylum had walked down this same street and been inspired.

Skylar was already examining the fantastical creations cluttering a nearby table. One caught

Aldwyn's eye as well. It was a small chest with eight magical wands affixed to it like legs.

"Curious, are you?" the vendor asked Aldwyn. He looked like a cave troll, with ears the size of a small elephant's. "I call it a wandling."

The vendor laid a coin down on the table. The chest sprang to life, scurrying like a spider over to the piece of silver. Once it arrived, the wandling opened its lid and swallowed the coin whole.

"It's an automaton," the vendor continued. "Neither alive nor inanimate. You never have to feed it and it's always at your service. Both protecting small treasures and collecting new ones."

The vendor shuffled over to a hooded customer browsing on the other side of the booth. Aldwyn walked up to Gilbert, who also had taken an interest in a contraption: a mechanical box that spat out decorated confections when a lever was pulled. Gilbert took a peek inside to see how it worked, but as his face got closer, a square of chocolate mousse shot out of the machine and splattered across his forehead.

Aldwyn allowed himself just another moment

to observe a bubbling cauldron. Inside, a spoon was stirring the stew of ingredients without the need of any hand to grip its handle.

Aldwyn walked back over to where the vendor was talking to the hooded customer.

"Excuse me," Aldwyn said. "I hope you can answer my question. I'm searching for a remwalker. Do you know of any around here?"

"I am an Appnian," the vendor replied. "Born of this world and content to never leave it. Remwalkers are my people, too, but their curiosity about Vastia and the Beyond is so great they have made it their calling to assist visitors such as yourselves. Really they just want you to stay so they can leave in your place."

"You didn't answer my question," Aldwyn said.

"Go back the way you came, past the River of Teeth," the vendor replied. "There's a shack deep in the Mud Basins. You'll find some Red Eyes there."

Aldwyn nodded and caught up with Skylar and Gilbert, who were looking at another peddler's wares, amazing potions of a thousand colors. A list of ingredients was stuck with slug goo to each beaker. Skylar was studying one of the magic recipes.

"Bad news, I'm afraid," Aldwyn said. "The vendor says if we want to find a remwalker, we've traveled the wrong way. It's back down to the ground for us."

"This is a goose chase if I've ever seen one," Skylar huffed.

Just then a voice from behind them spoke: "Appnians have a tendency to tell lies, especially about remwalkers."

The familiars turned to see the hooded customer—a young woman with pale skin and bloodshot eyes.

"I overheard you talking," she said. "I can help you. What is it you're looking for here?"

"The Palace of Dreams," Aldwyn said. "Queen Loranella's life is in danger, and she is the only one with the knowledge to save herself."

"I see," the remwalker replied. "The palace is far from here. I've been once before. But I assure you the route I took no longer exists today."

"Then how will you get us there?" Skylar asked.

"Few are able to track the chaotic patterns of the Dreamworld. Lucky for you, I know someone who can. We'll visit him and he will show us the way."

Aldwyn looked to Skylar and Gilbert. They would all be proceeding with caution, but that was nothing new for the trio. They followed behind the remwalker, who was moving swiftly through the twisted streets.

"That building, up ahead," Aldwyn said. "I could have sworn we passed the exact same one already."

"The city changes, same as the clouds in your world," the remwalker replied. "Drifting together and apart. You'll see it more clearly once we reach the outskirts."

"How do you not go crazy living in a place like this?" Aldwyn asked.

"It's the only place I've ever known. But I long to visit the world you come from."

"So why don't you?" Gilbert asked.

"Some remwalkers have tried. They've attempted to escape through the dreaming rug portals of those they helped guide here. But something in the

Dreamworld holds fast the ones born within it. Somebody would have to willingly take our place. I don't believe any from your land have made that bargain yet."

Aldwyn could see why. It was like being stuck in a dream you couldn't wake up from. He was already starting to question his sanity, and he hadn't even been there long.

"Why aren't any of you carrying the string from your rug?" the remwalker asked.

"Our rug was destroyed," Skylar replied.

"Then how will you leave us?" the remwalker asked.

"We thought we'd deal with one crisis at a time," Aldwyn said. "And right now the more urgent one is getting to the queen."

They reached the far edge of the city, where the big cloud they were on tapered off into islands of smaller ones. On each new cloud Aldwyn could see buildings floating, disconnected from the dream metropolis.

"The tracker we seek lives up there," the remwalker said, indicating a house sitting atop one of the wisps of white.

"Is there a staircase I'm not seeing?" Gilbert asked. "Another ladder in the trees?"

"No, nothing like that this time," the remwalker answered.

She approached a metal post. It had a translucent string tied to it that Aldwyn wouldn't have noticed without the remwalker. She grabbed hold of the string and pulled it taut. With another tug, she began reeling in the island like a loose kite in the wind. Aldwyn, Skylar, and Gilbert watched as the remwalker dragged the cloud with the tracker's house closer.

Soon, the remwalker had brought the cloud island to within a step of the familiars, and she tightened the line so it couldn't float away. Aldwyn, Skylar, and Gilbert were easily able to cross from the gravel road they were standing on to the one paving the cloud.

They were close enough to see the tracker's house now, which looked no bigger than a one-horse barn. The remwalker approached the front door and knocked. The door swung open to reveal an old man. His eyes were so red and so deep that Aldwyn couldn't even see the pupils.

"Hello, Papa," the remwalker said. "I need to borrow the Atlas."

Without blinking, he stepped aside, allowing them all to enter.

"It's not a good time to travel," the old man said. "Night is coming."

"They don't have the luxury of waiting," the remwalker replied.

"Very well, then," the man said.

He led them inside the room. There was no bed. Nowhere to sleep. Just maps covering the walls. And a tome at the room's center so huge it would take all of one man's strength to turn the pages. It was as large as an ocean raft.

The remwalker stood before the massive book, which Aldwyn could safely assume was the Atlas. There must have been a hundred tabs, each a different color. The remwalker located the one that was maroon, then gave a heave, flipping the book open to a sprawling, three-dimensional map that seemed as alive as the world outside. The rivers flowed like real water and the illustrated trees blew as if they were in the wind.

The remwalker stepped across the Atlas, past mountains and making sure not to get her feet wet in the lakes. She found the Palace of Dreams hovering inside a glass ball.

"It's just like in my dream," Aldwyn said.

"Those mountains will be uncrossable for the animals," the old man told his daughter. "Even you won't make it." Then he gestured to a large door carved into the side of the mountain range. "You'll have to gain Elzzup's permission to pass through his tunnels."

"There must be another way," the remwalker said. "The Dreamworld will surely shift again before we arrive."

"I've been watching," the old man said. "The mountains moved just a few hours ago. They'll remain steady at least until morning. And besides, you don't have that long anyway. You have to be out by midnight."

The remwalker nodded, then turned to the familiars.

"What does he mean?" Gilbert asked.

"After midnight, things change here," she said.

"How exactly?" Aldwyn asked.

The remwalker looked to her father.

"That's when the Dreamworld turns into a nightmare," the old man said.

14

TO THE MOUNTAIN

The familiars stood on a hillside just beyond the Forest of Ladders, awaiting the remwalker's next move. In the soft glow of the moonlight, she was staring out through a spyglass at the mountains in the distance.

"It looks like a straight path from here," Skylar said.

"Your eye is not trained to see what I see," the remwalker replied, lowering the spyglass. "We'll go that way," she added, pointing away from the mountain range to a tangle of jungle and forest.

"I don't understand," Aldwyn said.

"The direct route will have us traveling in circles

and never getting anywhere. I've been through the jungle before. I know its tricks."

The remwalker returned the spyglass to her satchel and headed west. Aldwyn, Skylar, and Gilbert followed.

"Why are you helping us, anyway?" Skylar asked. "You've never even asked who we are."

"It's not important to me," the remwalker replied. "What you've done in your past or where you've been. Whether you're penniless or as rich as a king. It's not *who* you are that counts. It's *what* you are. And I can see that the three of you are pure of heart."

Aldwyn considered her words. It was a lovely sentiment, one that might have even been true in the Dreamworld. But in the real world, nothing was ever that simple.

"Have Appnians always lived here?" Gilbert asked.

"Not always. For thousands of years, it was inhabited only by those who dreamed. Our people came much, much later. The Appnians lived on a small peninsula across the Wildecape Sea. They were fishermen and farmers. Life for them was wonderful. They worked during the day and celebrated their bounties at night. They rested just enough to give them energy for the next day. Life was so good they didn't want to sleep it away.

"Then everything changed. Barbaro al-Reqi, a warlord from the Colharp tribe, led an invasion. Once his army had conquered this new territory, they enslaved the Appnians, forcing the men to work tirelessly, building ships and armor.

"The one place where those who survived could escape the hardship was in their dreams. They believed their only chance at happiness was to dream permanently. A circle of elder women responsible for making the sails prayed to the moon gods for some guidance on how to do this. Their answer came in beams of silk that poured down from the sky. The next morning they began weaving them into a blanket with a swirling pattern at its center.

"Barbaro thought it was just another sail for his ships. He never knew what the elders were planning until it was too late. One night, after the blanket was complete, every man, woman, and child of Appnia gathered atop it. They closed their eyes and disappeared forever.

"When the warlord awoke to find his slaves were all gone, he was enraged. He had no idea where they had gone until that night, when he slept. For in his dreams, all the Appnians were there, more than happy to torment him.

"Believing the blanket to be the only explanation, he shred it to pieces. All the tiny threads were caught up in the wind, and when wizards discovered them, they used those very same threads to weave together the dreaming rugs you use today.

"There are many Appnians, like my father, who long to stay in the Dreamworld forever. But some of us still wish to see the outside, no matter how brutal it can be."

The group's journey to the tangle of jungle and forest was, as Aldwyn expected, a strange one. A field of fingers rose up from the ground like blades of grass, wiggling. Aldwyn gently tiptoed across them, but the remwalker was far less delicate with her footfalls. She was cracking knuckles with each stomp of her boot.

Aldwyn had taken only a few steps inside the forest when he saw a horrifying fanged beast dart past, chasing a young girl into the dark. The sound of feet breaking branches echoed from every direction. Dreamers all around them were running for their lives.

"What is this place?" Aldwyn asked.

"This is where the things that go bump in the night reside," the remwalker said. "When you have dreams of being chased, it's often through here."

They continued forward, deeper into the tangle of trees and darkness, where all manner of bogeymen roamed.

"There's nothing to be afraid of," the remwalker said. "It's fear that these creatures feed on. So long as they don't sense any cowardice, you'll be safe."

"Easy for you to say," Gilbert muttered.

From above, an owl as large as a dragon swooped down, pursuing a small finch. But it stopped in mid-flight and turned its attention to the familiars instead.

"Gilbert, get ahold of yourself," Aldwyn said. "We just have to make it out of the forest."

Gilbert looked confused.

"It's not Gilbert who's scared," Skylar said. "It's me."

The giant owl was hungrily eyeing all three animals.

"Follow me," the remwalker said. "We better hurry."

She took off running. Aldwyn, Skylar, and Gilbert followed. The owl beat its wings behind them, knocking small trees over as it flew. The remwalker seemed to know her way through the dark maze, hurdling fallen logs and dodging jagged roots to reach a boulder hidden in the trees. She grabbed at a crack, and pulled a door open. The familiars hurried inside. The owl soared past.

The boulder had been hollowed out and a flame fairy danced above a small campfire to warm anyone who sought out this place for refuge.

As they caught their breath, Aldwyn asked Skylar, "Why were you so afraid back there?"

"That creature. I've seen it in my own dreams before. When I was barely out of the nest. At the Aviary, the older birds called it the nightflyer. They told stories about how it would catch fledglings in their sleep. Pluck their feathers one by one before swallowing them whole. Just the thought of it makes me shudder."

"Then stop thinking about it," the remwalker said. "More than anything, these monsters of the forest smell weakness."

Skylar attempted to gather herself, to regain her usual calm. But the sound of scratching and scraping could be heard against the outside of the boulder. It was clear she was still shaken.

"Dreams, especially the bad ones, have a way of haunting us," the remwalker said. "And because they reoccur, sometimes over and over, they can feel more real than your waking life."

The nightflyer tore the door open with its claws, splintering the boulder and exposing the four huddled inside. The remwalker reached into her satchel and pulled out a blowgun. She lifted it to her mouth, pursed her lips around one end, and fired. A capsule of powder struck the giant owl in the face, exploding into a spray of blinding sand. The beast let out a screech and retreated. But the nightflyer's cry alerted all the other creatures of the dark that there was an enemy in their midst.

The group fled from the broken boulder, taking off at top speed. Aldwyn had never seen Skylar move quite so fast before. A gelatinous blob lunged out from a hole in the ground, attempting to swallow Gilbert, but the tree frog hopped behind a rock just in time. More monsters began charging from all around, everything from giant wolves to skeletal dragons.

"You may not like what I'm about to do," the remwalker stated. "But no harm will come of it."

She stuck out her foot and tripped a passing dreamer, causing him to stumble and fall. The boy's eyes went wide with terror, and all the monsters converged on him, allowing the remwalker and the familiars to run away.

Aldwyn looked back, wanting to help.

"Don't be a fool," the remwalker said. "I already told you, those who visit the Dreamworld in their sleep can't be harmed. You, however, can be killed."

It pained Aldwyn to hear the boy's cries, but he knew the remwalker was right.

They arrived at the end of the jungle and exited the brush to find that they were closer to the mountains than Aldwyn thought possible, especially since they hadn't been heading in that direction at all. From here he could see the carved door to Elzzup's tunnel. It couldn't have been more than a mile away. Of course, what appeared to be a mile in this world could be anything but.

"Guys, look over there!" Gilbert exclaimed.

His excitement wasn't due to the fact that they had escaped that terrible forest. It was because of what he saw up ahead: Anura swimming in a pool of maggots.

Gilbert was hopping as fast as his legs would carry him.

"Anura!" he shouted.

The golden toad turned to him. "Gilbert, have you come to swim?"

"I'm not dreaming," Gilbert said. "I'm really here. Aldwyn and Skylar, too."

Anura looked over to see them.

"I must have dozed off while sitting at the queen's bedside," Anura said.

"How is she?" Gilbert asked.

"Getting weaker by the hour. My good luck is failing her." As she spoke, the maggots in the pool began to drain away. "I fear that I'm waking. Is there anything I can do?"

"Just let her know that she's going to be okay," Gilbert said. "Tell her we won't let her down."

The last maggots disappeared from the pool, leaving an empty ditch. Anura vanished a moment later. Gilbert returned to his companions' sides.

"We won't let her down," Gilbert repeated. "Will we?"

"We've always come through before," Aldwyn said.

Just then, a charge of wand-wielding wizards dressed in Turnbuckle Academy uniforms emerged from the forest. They each had yarn from a rug tied around their wrists. The group was led by a pair of remwalkers, who stepped aside upon seeing the cat, bird, and frog.

"I knew our loyals would be overpowered sooner or later," Aldwyn said. "But if they've hurt Jack, they'll be sorry."

"We could run for the mountain door," the remwalker said, "but Elzzup will have a test for you. Something to challenge your wits. You'll have no hope of passing it if you're under attack from those wizards."

"So what do you suggest?" Aldwyn asked.

"Stand your ground. Face them head-on."

The Turnbuckle students were getting closer, crossing the empty pool of maggots.

"We're outnumbered, and I fear our magic can't be counted on in the Dreamworld," Skylar said.

"Surely you've relied on talents other than your magic in the past," the remwalker said.

For Aldwyn, it wasn't so long ago that other talents were *all* he had to rely on. He thought back to what he did to survive on the streets of Bridgetower. He had to be clever. Use the elements he had around him to tip the odds in his favor. Aldwyn scanned his surroundings and his eyes landed on a metal post similar to the one that had tethered the cloud holding the tracker's house. He looked closely and saw that it, too, had a translucent string attached to it, stretching high up into the clouds.

The Turnbuckle students were aiming their wands and were well within striking distance.

"You can either come back willingly or suffer the consequences of not coming back at all," one of the students warned.

Aldwyn turned to Skylar and Gilbert.

"Run toward them," he said. "Then scramble. Around their legs, between them. Don't waste your time attacking. And whatever you do, don't get caught."

"We're facing death and capture, and you suggest a glorified game of tag?" Skylar asked.

"Just trust me," Aldwyn replied.

He sprinted for the oncoming wizards. Gilbert and Skylar went in different directions. The Turnbuckle spellcasters were unprepared for this counterintuitive tactic. They began chasing the animals, but the familiars were running circles around them. Two of the young wizards pursued Aldwyn.

"Hold your fire," one shouted to the other, lowering his wand. "An errant blast could take off a hand, or worse."

He wasn't the only one taking precautions. His fellow students were being just as careful.

"Aldwyn, care to share your brilliant plan anytime soon?" Skylar asked.

But Aldwyn didn't need to answer. A Turnbuckle pupil tripped over the dreaming rug yarn of another, setting off a chain reaction. One young wizard after another fell, until they were all in a heap. Aldwyn used his telekinesis to untie the translucent string attached to the metal post and retie it to the ball of yarn entangling the students. When the next strong breeze blew in, the cloud above—no longer tethered to the metal post— began to drift away, tugging the entire crumpled mess of fallen wizards and yarn along with it.

Some tried to tear themselves free. Others sent bolts from their wands. But Aldwyn, Skylar, Gilbert, and the remwalker merely watched as Turnbuckle's finest floated off into the distance. The wizards were still in sight when the entire knotty ball of them vanished instantly, leaving the translucent string and cloud flying freely.

"What just happened?" Gilbert asked.

"I'm not sure," the remwalker replied.

"Perhaps they entered this world in their sleep," Skylar said.

"They wouldn't have been carrying their dreaming rug yarn if that was the case," the remwalker said.

The four stood there, dumbfounded for the moment.

"Congratulations," a voice called out from behind them. "You interest me."

The group turned to see a possum, not much bigger than Aldwyn. He had gray fur, coal-black eyes, and a long pink tail. A slender necklace hung around his neck, with a cube of silver dangling from it.

"Elzzup," the remwalker said. "We were coming to see you."

"I know. That's why I challenged you with that first puzzle. Needless to say, those students weren't real. The attack was just a little brainteaser to get you warmed up."

"An illusion?" Skylar asked.

"No, different than that," Elzzup replied. "This cube I wear around my neck is a piece taken from the Dreamworld's creation stone. It's the last of its kind. With it, I have the power to conjure into existence whatever I please."

"Sounds like you just enjoy tormenting people," Aldwyn said.

"You should be happy," Elzzup continued. "Those who don't pass my first test never even see the inside of my castle. That's where the real fun begins."

Elzzup headed for the great door carved into the mountainside. The familiars kept pace behind.

"Should you succeed in the tasks ahead, your journey to the Palace of Dreams will continue on the other side of my castle walls. But if you fail, you will be my prisoners. To have the Prophesized Three as my prize, what could be sweeter?"

"Sounds like an expensive toll," Aldwyn said.

"Well, I make the rules of this game," Elzzup said. "If you want to play, follow me."

Elzzup entered into the torch-lit tunnel beyond the door. Aldwyn, Skylar, and Gilbert paused before the threshold. They looked to the remwalker.

"You never mentioned anything about imprisonment," Skylar said.

"If you truly want to reach the Palace of Dreams, this passage is your only hope," the remwalker replied.

The familiars considered her words, then marched forward into Elzzup's lair.

15

ELZZUP'S PUZZLE

As the giant doors closed behind Aldwyn, Skylar, Gilbert, and the remwalker, the light cast from the moon quickly disappeared, leaving only the flickering glow from the torches on the wall to guide them forward. Elzzup was leading the way, waddling ahead without so much as a glance back at his guests.

Drops were falling from above, landing on Aldwyn's fur, but he couldn't make out the source in the dark.

"What is that?" Aldwyn asked.

"Feels like some kind of dew," Gilbert replied.

Upon passing the next torch, Aldwyn was able

to see more clearly overhead.

"That's not water, Gilbert," he said. "That's bat drool!"

Hundreds of cave bats hung from the ceiling, with mouths open and goo dripping from their fangs. Aldwyn shook his fur but the slime wouldn't come off that easily.

The tunnel sloped downward, and the temperature cooled as they descended. Dark eyes glared out from every corner. It was impossible to tell what each creature was, but the sound of growling stomachs made Aldwyn less than eager to find out.

"Don't worry about them," Elzzup said. "They don't feed until after midnight."

The familiars hurried, and it wasn't long before they were entering a cavern large enough to house a small city. Rising up from the ground were limestone stalagmites that had been hollowed out and carved into a series of buildings connected by rope bridges. Even more dramatic were the stalactites that hung from the cave ceiling. Both top and bottom seemed to be inhabited. Together, the structures from above and below formed a castle of unfathomable beauty.

"You said something about a game," Aldwyn remarked. "When can we start?"

"How can you be so sure that the game hasn't already begun?" Elzzup asked.

Aldwyn hated to be toyed with, but they were at the mercy of the possum's whims. Elzzup walked through the castle door and closed it before the others had a chance to enter behind him.

"What's the meaning of this?" Skylar asked. "Let us in."

"I will only open it after you answer me this. When is a door not a door?" Elzzup called out from inside.

"When it's in pieces!" Gilbert shouted. "Which is exactly what it's going to be if you don't open it right now."

A mocking snicker could be heard from the other side.

"Gilbert, I've never seen you lose your temper like that," Aldwyn said.

"I'm not myself on an empty stomach," Gilbert replied.

"Fitting, given the possum's riddle," Skylar said. "When is a door not itself?"

"When it's hungry?" Gilbert asked.

"What else could a door be used for?" Skylar asked. "You can put legs on it and make it a table." She addressed Elzzup through the closed door. "When it's a table."

This time only silence greeted them.

"You must understand who you're dealing with here," the remwalker said. "Most animals view the world right side up. But a possum like Elzzup looks at things differently. Upside down is the norm."

"I don't know about the rest of you, but I sure could use some brain food right now," Gilbert said. "Any chance I could find a jar of fruit flies around here?"

"That's it, Gilbert," Aldwyn said.

"Really? Fruit flies?" the tree frog replied.

"No," Aldwyn said. "A jar." He turned to the door. "A door is not a door when it is ajar."

There was a long pause. Then the door opened, wide enough for them all to enter.

Inside the stalagmite palace, the floor was made not from stone tiles but interlocking puzzle pieces.

"Being a possum has little to do with my fondness for puzzles," Elzzup said. "I traveled to this world just as you did, on a dreaming rug. I came alongside my loyal. We were Beyonders, bored by the routine of life in Vastia. Here things changed every day, every hour. We agreed that we would stay here forever. But then she changed her mind. I refused to go back with her, to the dull land you call home. After time, though, even the randomness of the Dreamworld became predictable. So now I entertain myself by toying with those passing through. Folks like you."

Elzzup scurried ahead and darted around a corner. By the time the familiars and the remwalker caught up, the possum was gone. The group kept moving forward until they reached a large room with a hole at its top. What appeared to be sunlight streamed in. Not far from Aldwyn, the rays struck a prism, splitting into five beams of multicolored light. Each sliver of color shined down a different darkened passageway.

Suddenly Elzzup spoke.

"You'll have to do a better job of keeping up. Otherwise you're going to get left behind. Now if you hope to find me, let the sun guide you."

Another riddle. Aldwyn knew that choosing the right path would require careful thinking. He looked before him and saw that a picture was painted above the archway to each corridor. A beam of red light stretched beneath a picture of a horse. A beam of orange beneath one of a mother and child. Yellow to a tree. Purple to a king. And blue to a lion and tiger.

"This is impossible," Gilbert cried. "The light goes in every direction!"

"Maybe we should be focused on the different colors," Aldwyn said. "Sunlight is orange, so perhaps that's the path we should take."

"I always thought the sun was yellow," Gilbert said.

"And neither of you is taking into account the time of day," the remwalker added. "At sunset, the light is red, or even purple."

"Well, trees need sunlight to live," Gilbert said. "So that's another check for yellow. Puzzle solved."

He started hopping toward the corridor. The moment Gilbert crossed beneath the archway, a bed of spikes came hurtling down. Aldwyn used his telekinesis to tug Gilbert out of the way, just a split second before the tree frog would have been impaled in fifty different places.

"Puzzles never really were my thing," Gilbert said.

"The next time we might not be so lucky," Aldwyn said.

"Maybe Gilbert was onto something by thinking about the pictures," Skylar said. "Horse, mother and child, tree, king—"

"Wait," Aldwyn interrupted. "Does that child look like a girl or boy?"

"A boy," Skylar answered. "Why?"

"Because that would make him the woman's *son*," Aldwyn said.

Gilbert and Skylar nodded, and they all followed the orange light to the passageway. No spikes came rushing down from above. The group continued up a staircase that led to a room at the peak of the stalactites. Elzzup was standing beside a pedestal with a delighted look on his face.

"Well done," the possum said. "You've already

made it farther than most."

Aldwyn and his companions walked closer.

"How many of these puzzles will we have to solve before you let us out of here?" Aldwyn asked.

"Just two more," Elzzup replied. "Now look above you."

The familiars and remwalker turned their gaze upward. The ceiling was cone shaped, its highest point directly above the pedestal, hundreds of feet in the air.

"Your next challenge is to determine the precise height of this room, but you will only have one tool to help you find your answer." Elzzup gestured to a knife resting atop the pedestal. "This five-inch knife."

The possum stepped back, leaving the group to ponder.

"Skylar, you can measure the distance," Gilbert suggested. "Or, Aldwyn, you can use your telekinesis to move the knife five inches at a time."

"It would be impossible to get an accurate reading," Aldwyn replied. "We'd be guessing in the end, and never get the answer right."

"There's a mathematical way to solve this,"

Skylar said. "Measure the distance from the center point of the room to the outer wall, then the distance along the wall from the bottom point to the top. If you square that distance and then subtract the square distance of the previous measurement, and then you take the square root of that, you'll have your answer."

Aldwyn and Gilbert just stared at her.

"Yeah, good luck with that," the tree frog said.

"What? It's simple trigonometry," Skylar replied.

"We're still relying on the accuracy of those measurements," Aldwyn said. "If one is even the slightest bit off, we'll fail."

They appeared stumped. Elzzup grinned, observing from nearby.

"I think you may be using this tool in the wrong way," the remwalker said. She walked over to the pedestal and picked up the knife in her hand. "It's not really meant for measuring anything."

The remwalker took a few steps toward Elzzup and put the knife to the possum's throat.

"Why don't you just tell us the answer," she threatened. "Or I could make you."

262

"Excellent," Elzzup said, clapping his hands. "Let's move on, shall we?"

The remwalker lowered the knife and Elzzup continued to the other side of the room. Aldwyn and the others followed.

"I guess when math fails, there's always stabbing," Gilbert said.

"I'm not sure that's the lesson to take away from that," Skylar replied.

"This is the final room within my castle," Elzzup said, coming to a chamber with three separate pathways leading onward. "Should you solve this last riddle, you will be free. All you must do is choose the correct pathway. There's only one way out that won't end in death. So choose wisely."

Aldwyn stared at the three paths leading forward. He watched as a trio of chained beasts emerged. In the first pathway stood a spider the size of an elephant. Its rows upon rows of fangs were chomping hungrily at the air. In the second was a small, gentle-looking woodland raccoon. And in the third a sleeping black-tooth dragon.

"We've still got this knife," the remwalker said, never having let the weapon go.

"And that raccoon seems nice," Gilbert added.

"Remember what Kalstaff always said," Skylar remarked. "Oft times, the friendliest-looking creatures are the ones that are most dangerous."

"Only one way out won't end in death," Aldwyn repeated.

"I think it's clear what choice we have to make," Skylar said.

Gilbert nodded his head and started walking toward the raccoon.

"The black-tooth dragon," Skylar continued.

Gilbert froze in his tracks.

"Are you kidding?" he asked. "Deadly poison dripping from its teeth. Without the Mountain Alchemist's sleeping powder, that would be suicide."

"We've defeated a dragon like this one before," Skylar said. "I always prefer facing the enemy I know over those I don't."

"There has to be a certain answer," Aldwyn said. "We can't just go on intuition. It's a trick. Something we're not considering."

"Maybe there's a secret passageway out of here,

or a trapdoor of some kind," Skylar said.

They started searching the chamber, feeling the floor and walls for any inconsistencies. Once again, Elzzup watched, wringing his paws in anticipation.

"It doesn't seem like there's any other way out," Aldwyn said. "Just these three paths, and the way we came in, of course."

"What if that's the answer?" Gilbert asked. "We don't go forward. We go back."

Aldwyn thought about it for a moment. It did make sense.

"There's only one way out that won't end in death," Skylar said yet again. "Elzzup never said that it had to be one of these paths."

The four of them turned their backs to the chained beasts and started for the chamber's entrance, leaving Elzzup behind. They headed toward the cone-shaped room and found that instead of going back to where they'd been, the path led them straight out of the castle, through a passage that deposited them on the other side of the mountain. The stars of the night sky glimmered above them. Stranger still, Elzzup was already standing there.

"You proved yourselves quite up to the challenge of my games," the possum said. "But I've always been a bit of a sore loser."

Suddenly, the elephant spider, raccoon, and black-tooth dragon were standing behind him. The beasts began closing in on the familiars and the remwalker. Even though Aldwyn was feeling nervous, he wouldn't show it.

"That's the best you can do?" the street-smart cat asked.

"I can do whatever I want," Elzzup replied, stroking his necklace. "With this cube, my powers are limitless."

"Powerful enough to create something that even your necklace couldn't destroy?" Aldwyn asked.

"If I wanted."

"I don't believe it," Aldwyn said.

"Aldwyn, we're trying to get rid of monsters, not make more of them," Gilbert said.

Elzzup clutched the cube and another creature rose up from the ground, this one bigger, stronger, meaner, and uglier than the rest. Its arms were made of rock and mud, tentacles stretched from its mouth, and sharp horns protruded from its head.

"Do you doubt me now?" Elzzup asked boastfully.

"No," Aldwyn said.

Just then, the beast lowered a huge, stomping foot atop the possum's head, crushing him and the cube necklace instantly. There was no way the necklace could destroy the monster now. It turned to the spider, raccoon, and dragon, and as they fought one another, Aldwyn and his companions made a run for safety.

"Did you see what that thing did to Elzzup?" Gilbert asked, still shaken.

"I've heard of possums playing dead before, but that gives the saying a whole new meaning," Skylar replied.

They looked back to see that the raccoon was the only one who was holding his own, having grown to ten times its size and burst into flames. The remwalker led them across the flatlands, and in the distance Aldwyn could see the reflective surface of the glass ball housing the Palace of Dreams and a flurry of snowflakes.

"That's it," Aldwyn said. "That's where I saw the queen."

He only hoped she was still there now and that she had the answers they had come looking for.

16

MIDNIGHT

Unlike in Vastia, where the desert sand cooled after sundown, here in the Dreamworld it remained hot all night long. The pads on the bottoms of Aldwyn's feet were proof of that, scalding and burning with every step. It made the sight of snowflakes falling within the glass ball all the odder.

They arrived outside the glass and stared up at the palace, which was hovering in midair. There was just one little problem: there was no way through the glass.

"I thought we were finished with puzzles," Aldwyn said.

"The answers are never easy," the remwalker replied. "But there must be a way inside."

"And I think I know just what that is," Aldwyn said, pointing to a field of dandelions nearby.

"Planning to smell your way in?" Skylar asked.

"It was in my dream," Aldwyn said. "Remember, just like I told you. I sunk into the field and ended up inside the palace."

Aldwyn walked over and the others followed. As he stepped through the field of yellow flowers, petals began to brush up against his ankles. He didn't know where exactly his feet would start to sink, so he just kept walking deeper into the field. Skylar flapped over, setting her talons on the ground. Gilbert hopped about, stomping his feet on the earth as if that might help make it open up for them. But nothing seemed to be working.

"Maybe there's another waaaaaay," Aldwyn said as his feet began to sink. He didn't even get a chance to watch the others go under. For a moment everything went dark. Then Aldwyn was inside the glass ball, drifting downward atop one of the snowflakes. His companions were nowhere to be seen.

When he touched down, he found himself just outside the palace walls, not far from the staircase he had ascended in his dream. He looked up to the second-story balcony, but Queen Loranella wasn't standing there waiting for him.

"Skylar!" Aldwyn called out. "Gilbert! Can you hear me?"

His cries merely echoed back to him.

Aldwyn began wandering around, looking for his friends or a way inside the palace. He started moving with a greater sense of urgency. And as much as he wanted to be reunited with his friends, his main concern was still for the queen.

He spotted a gate in the palace wall and a small series of steps that led up to it. He quickly climbed them and slid through the entrance. Once inside, everything looked very familiar. Aldwyn knew the way to the queen's chamber, at least he did in the real world. He ran through the courtyard and up the palace staircase. Aldwyn could feel his heart racing. He was getting so close to an answer. Too close to fall short now.

He ran through the upstairs hall, front feet then back. There was still no sign of Gilbert,

Skylar, or the remwalker, but finding them would have to wait. He could hear the queen's enchanted harp playing softly in her room.

Aldwyn reached her door and pushed his way inside. The bed was empty. He darted his head to see Loranella standing, alive and well.

"Aldwyn," she said. "I was hoping you'd find me."

"We got here as fast as we could," Aldwyn said.

"We?" the queen asked.

"Skylar and Gilbert. They're here, too. Well, they were. I sort of lost them." Loranella looked at him curiously. "I have so much to tell you. At your party, we gave you a gift."

"I remember."

"It was cursed, with a parasitic poison. Everyone thinks we were responsible. That we tried to kill you."

"Someone must have gone to a lot of trouble to frame you, then," the queen said.

"Who would want you dead?" Aldwyn asked.

"I have no idea. I've made my fair share of enemies over the years. Do you have any clues?"

"Well, for one, the Mountain Alchemist is

dead. We visited the Turn to try and contact him in the Tomorrowlife, but a spell vacuum had been cast over the spot to keep him from us. Oh, and his only book, the thirteenth volume of Parnabus McCallister's Divining Spells, had been taken, too. We went to Turnbuckle Academy to look for something in Kalstaff's old journals, but the pages had been torn out. And that wasn't all. Yajmada's armor, the one he kept in his cottage cellar, it was missing as well."

The queen paced the room.

"You said you visited the Turn. While you were there, did you see the monument? There should have been a gem within the plaque."

"The monument was shattered, the gem gone," Aldwyn said. It was clear that the queen had figured something out. "Why? What is it?"

"Yajmada's armor is one of the most powerful weapons of destruction ever created. But only when the four storm diamonds are all in place. After Wyvern and Skull were defeated, Kalstaff, the Mountain Alchemist, and I each took one of the diamonds. The fourth was hidden inside the monument at the Turn. Someone is trying to collect them once more."

"What if they already have?" Aldwyn asked.

"For the sake of Vastia, let's hope that's not the case," she said. "You need to get me out of the Wander. I can't be of any use here."

"That's why I've come," Aldwyn said. "You're the only one who knows how to re-create Somnibus Everwake's remedy for a parasitic poison. You must tell me so I can return to the outside world and get it to you before it's too late."

"Yes, of course."

Loranella retrieved a quill pen from a small writing table and began to transcribe the spell's ingredients from memory. All forty-three of them.

"I've felt like a prisoner in my own palace walls," she said as she wrote. "I'm starting to lose track of time here. How long have I been trapped like this?"

"Almost three days now," Aldwyn said. "There isn't much time. I should go. I still need to find a way out of this place. And Skylar and Gilbert."

She handed him the scrap of parchment and then took him by the paw.

"Aldwyn, you need to be very careful. Whoever did this to me, whoever framed you, is very dangerous. Once they possess Yajmada's armor and the four storm diamonds, there will be no way to stop them."

"There was one more thing," Aldwyn said. "A message written to me while I was being kept in the dungeon beneath the palace. It said, 'Spuowbip wjots sby udpjbm uosdwoyt.' Does that mean anything to you?"

She considered for a moment.

"I'm sorry. No."

"We entered the Dreamworld through a dreaming rug, but we won't be able to escape through the same portal," Aldwyn said. "Do you know of any other way back to Vastia?"

"I took precautions on a visit here many moons ago," Loranella replied. "In case I was ever trapped with no other way to escape, I hid a dreaming rug. It's beyond the glass ball, by the glyphstone."

"And what about getting out of the palace?" Aldwyn asked.

"Just as you found your way in, you'll find your way out," she said. "See you when I'm awake."

Aldwyn gave her a final glance, then bounded for the door. He raced back for the palace exit with the parchment held between his teeth. Once outside, he returned to the top of the same steps he had ascended from the ground. From this high vantage point, Aldwyn was able to look out and see beyond the glass ball, to the dandelion field he sank into. There standing among the petals were Skylar, Gilbert, and the remwalker. It appeared that they had never left. He felt a flood of relief that they were safe, and now understood why he didn't see them within the palace. While Aldwyn had been able to use the dandelions to transport himself inside the glass ball, the same rules didn't apply to his companions.

Aldwyn raced down the steps and up to the glass wall nearest the field. He banged his paws against the clear divide.

"Gilbert! Skylar! Over here!"

When they saw Aldwyn, Skylar, Gilbert, and the remwalker hurried over.

"Did you find her?" Skylar called through the glass.

"She told us everything we need to know to

create the potion," Aldwyn replied, holding up the list. "Now I just need to figure a way out of here."

He looked at the snowflakes falling all around him, but had little idea of how they could be of any use to him. Aldwyn racked his brain. Maybe there was a way to break through the glass. But even the four of them together wouldn't be strong enough to do that. Although there just might have been something that was.

"Skylar," Aldwyn said. "I want you to cast an illusion of Elzzup, and make sure he's wearing the same necklace."

Skylar didn't ask any questions. She simply lifted her wings and summoned a replica of the now deceased possum before them.

"How exactly is this going to help get you out of there?" Gilbert asked.

Suddenly the ground began to tremble. Soon they saw a creature thundering out from behind the mountain. It was the giant beast that had crushed Elzzup. And it was heading straight for them.

"Skylar, move the illusion of Elzzup as close to the glass as you can," Aldwyn said.

As she did just that, Aldwyn darted underneath the outer palace steps to take cover. It was a good thing, too, because a moment later, the monster charged right through the illusion of Elzzup, slamming its horned head and shoulder into the glass wall. The glass shattered upon contact. Aldwyn curled himself into a ball as hundreds of shards of glass went flying in every direction.

Skylar sent the illusion of Elzzup running into the desert. The monster took off after it, and Aldwyn crawled out from under the steps. He carefully shook himself off and navigated through the fallen glass debris to his companions.

"Let's go see my father," the remwalker said. "He should be able to help you find another way back to the outside world."

"We won't have to go that far," Aldwyn said. "Queen Loranella told me she hid a dreaming rug by the glyphstone."

"I know where that is," the remwalker said. "We better hurry. It's almost midnight."

The desert was becoming populated with people, sleepers from Vastia and the Beyond. The

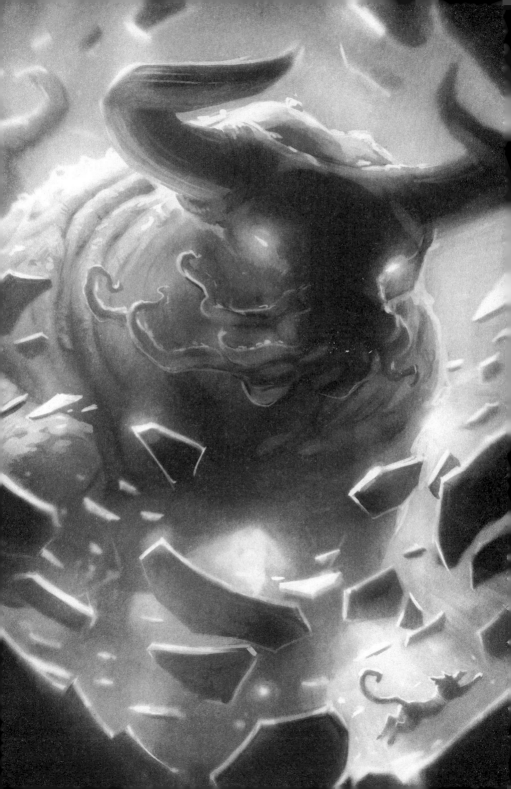

group quickened their pace, as all around them this world's nightmarish transformation began to take place. Worms and stinging ants rose up from the ground, slithering up the ankles and legs of any who passed. Aldwyn and Gilbert tried to brush away the creepy crawlers, but for every one they swatted off, three more took its place.

Skylar flew above the fray, but a thick cloud of biting flies enveloped the sky, casting a dark haze over everything in its path. Skylar was forced to drop down to the ground to avoid being swallowed. The remwalker had to cover her lips to keep the swarm from her mouth.

Panic was starting to erupt, with men, women, and animals desperate for a means of escape but finding none.

"This is awful," Gilbert said.

"It happens every night," the remwalker replied. "Appnians know to seek shelter. Those who dream have no choice but to endure this."

"Why?" Gilbert asked.

"No one is sure," the remwalker said. "Some think it is fueled by the fears that bubble up as we sleep."

Pushing through hordes of hysterical dreamers, Aldwyn spotted the broken remains of the glyphstone up ahead. Sheets of red rain fell from the sky, drenching the familiars and the remwalker. Upon reaching the crumbled stone, Aldwyn searched the rubble and found a rolled-up rug tucked into a hollow space.

"Over here," he called to the others.

They came up beside him as he used his mind to lay the dreaming rug flat on the ground. Just as Gilbert and Skylar were about to join Aldwyn atop the swirling pattern at the rug's center, the remwalker held the five-inch knife up to Gilbert's throat.

"I'm sorry I have to do this," she said. "But the only way I can leave is if one from your world takes my place here."

"So that's why you've gone to so much trouble to help us," Aldwyn said.

"I've wrestled with whether or not it would come to this," the remwalker said. "But I can't stay here any longer. I just want things to be the same, to stop changing."

Her bloodshot eyes looked more sad than angry.

"Hurting someone isn't the answer," Skylar reasoned. "We'll find another way to get you out. Put the knife down."

The remwalker's hand quivered but she wouldn't loosen her grip on the knife. Aldwyn telekinetically lifted one of the glyphstone fragments and cracked it across the back of her head. Her legs went limp beneath her and she fell to the dirt, unconscious.

"Come on," Aldwyn said. "Let's get out of here."

The three animals laid their heads on the rug and closed their eyes. Aldwyn felt a tug pulling him down into what felt like a viscous liquid, and when he paddled his way to the surface he was emerging out through a different rug into a small room. Skylar and Gilbert came up through the portal as well.

After he caught his breath, Aldwyn ran over to a nearby window. He used his mind to open the shutters, and when he peered out he was staring at a gold-and-silver-paved street.

They were back in Bronzhaven.

17

THE BUBBLING VIAL

"That leaves about thirty components," Skylar said.

She was perched on a table inside an abandoned cottage with the parchment listing the healing potion's ingredients laid out before her. Beside it, she had pulled more than a dozen components from her leather satchel.

"Luckily, I acquired some of the rarer ones from the Xylem garden," she said. "We'll need to get the rest from an apothecary."

"Why don't we just turn ourselves in to

Galatea?" Gilbert asked. "We can tell her what we've discovered and have the ravens and palace healers conjure the potion."

"What if we don't make it that far?" Aldwyn countered. "What if they lock us back up in the dungeons again? We can't risk it."

They turned to Skylar for the deciding vote.

"I'm sorry, Gilbert," she said. "We've already tried to reason with our closest allies, and look how that turned out. We need to see this through on our own."

"Once again, I'm the odd frog out," Gilbert said.

"There's an apothecary not far from here," Skylar continued. "It's where Sorceress Edna always picks up her mugwort. She says the alchemist there carries the freshest components this side of the Ebs."

"We're still fugitives, you know," Gilbert said. "By now, everyone in Vastia will be looking for us."

"We'll have to wait until the first sign of sun, travel under the guise of another one of Skylar's illusions, and take what we need," Aldwyn said. "If we save the queen, we'll be heroes again and all will be forgiven."

Skylar collected her things off the table, and the familiars rested their eyes and waited. A few hours passed before the earliest rays of light began creeping through the window. It was time. They exited the cottage into a quiet back alley.

"Skylar, lead the way," Aldwyn said.

Gilbert and Skylar returned to their perch on Aldwyn's back. The blue jay raised a wing and cast another illusion, making them again look like a bulldog.

"Go all the way to the end, then take the path along the edge of the park," Skylar said.

Aldwyn followed her directions, moving as quickly as he could through the alleyway before emerging onto the street. As he hurried along, he could see the townsfolk gathered around a horse cart, all dressed in yellow mourner's garb. They were holding vigil around a statue of Queen Loranella, which stood in the cart. It was covered in flowers. Slips of paper were tucked and folded into the floral arrangements. Some of the people were approaching the statue, placing valuables of their own all around it. Others chanted in unison, humming words in elvish. From the tired, defeated looks on their faces, they'd lost hope Loranella was on her way to recovery.

"Turn up there," Skylar said. "The apothecary's across the street."

Aldwyn spotted it, a small shop with a sign above the door that read "The Bubbling Vial." Beneath the name was a picture of a beaker that magically filled up with components and then boiled over before doing it again. A group of wizards entered and the familiars seized the opportunity to sneak in alongside them.

The shop was crowded with early morning customers, all browsing the alphabetized rows of glass jars. They were sniffing and examining each component before either placing it in their basket or returning it to the shelf. A middle-aged woman with a cane hobbled around the store selling her wares.

"I highly recommend the powdered rhubarb," the woman said to an elder sorcerer whose basket was already overflowing with goods. "Just got it in from the western border jungles last night. Perfect for conjuring phantom swords."

She turned to another customer.

"They should have everything we need," Skylar said, clutching the parchment in her talon. "Grab a basket."

Aldwyn used his mind to lift a wicker carrier and made it hover before them so it appeared that the illusion of the bulldog was actually holding the basket in its mouth.

"Let's start with the *As*," Skylar said. "Armadillo hair."

Aldwyn telekinetically opened a jar, removed a tuft of brown fur, and dropped it into the basket. Bark of everwillow and bumble wasp honey followed. Then copper chips and dew drops. Aldwyn mentally collected each one.

"Eye of snail," Skylar said, reading off the parchment.

Aldwyn added it to the basket. As they moved around the shop toward the *Fs*, the shop owner stepped in front of them.

"I don't believe I've seen you here before," the woman said. "Is there anything I can help you find?"

Skylar was quick to have the bulldog respond. "No, I'm fine, thanks."

287

"Well, if you have any questions, don't hesitate to ask."

The familiars hurried to gather the remaining components on the list. One by one they collected the ingredients for the healing potion. By the time they finished going through the entire alphabet, there was only a single component missing. They approached the shop owner, who was tidying up at the front counter.

Skylar made the dog appear to speak again. "Excuse us." She immediately realized her mistake. "Me. Excuse me. I didn't see any porcupine needles on the shelf."

"They've been in high demand of late," the woman replied. "Unfortunately all that's left has already been reserved."

Behind the counter, Aldwyn could see a locked cabinet with a vial of thin spikes stored inside.

"My apprentices should be bringing more back from the Thistle Meadow this week. I'd be happy to set some aside for you."

"That won't be necessary," Skylar said via the illusionary dog.

Aldwyn continued browsing, walking away from the counter.

"Now what?" Gilbert asked.

"We'll have to distract her," Skylar said. "I'll create another illusion. Aldwyn, use your telekinesis to lift the key and unlock that cabinet."

He nodded and Skylar raised a wing. On the opposite side of the shop, a dragonfly buzzed through an open window and began zipping around the customers. As they ducked and swatted, the store owner limped out from behind the counter, shooing at the insect with her cane. Aldwyn quickly turned his attention to the key ring dangling from her back pocket. He focused and mentally pulled the silver chain free.

While the lady was swinging at the dragonfly, Aldwyn used his mind to guide the key toward the tiny lock on the cabinet. He tried to line up the ridges inside the hole, but from his distance across the shop, the precise maneuver was too difficult to perform.

"What's taking you so long?" Skylar asked.

"I can't get it in," Aldwyn replied.

"Gilbert, go, now," Skylar said.

"What if she sees me?" Gilbert asked.

"Do it," Skylar insisted.

The tree frog leaped down from Aldwyn's back and hopped for the cabinet. The middle-aged woman was still too preoccupied with the dragonfly to see Gilbert bound over the counter and up to the cabinet. He swiped the key ring out of the air and used his webbed hand to slip it into the lock. With a quick turn it was open and the vial of porcupine needles was in his grasp.

Gilbert had made it only halfway back to the illusion of the bulldog when the store owner took a swing right through the dragonfly that sent her spinning. Once she regained her footing she was staring straight at Gilbert, who held the vial in his hand. The woman's eyes darted to the cabinet and she instantly knew what he had done.

"Thief!" the woman yelled, pointing at Gilbert.

The shop's customers, including the young wizards and elder sorcerer, turned.

"That's no ordinary thief," the sorcerer said. "That's one of the Prophesized Three."

The store owner flicked her wand at the bull-dog, shouting, *"Revelorsus!"*

The illusion disappeared, exposing Aldwyn and Skylar beneath.

"Stop them!" one of the wizards called. "They're the ones who tried to kill the queen."

The alchemist pointed her wand at the front door, slamming it. Aldwyn grabbed the basket of components in his teeth and started sprinting. Skylar flapped above him and Gilbert hopped behind. The Three made a dash for the open window and escaped just before the store owner's wand pulled it shut with a bang.

The familiars raced away from the shop. A moment later, the window behind them shattered as a messenger arrow cracked through the glass and went flying into the sky.

"We have to move fast," Aldwyn said to his companions. "Every one of the queen's soldiers will know where we are. And so will the Nightfall Battalion."

"We'll need a flame, a pot, and water to brew this healing potion," Skylar said.

"Marianne takes me to get soup at a small

inn around the corner from here," Gilbert said. "They don't start serving until after sundown. The kitchen should be empty now."

Skylar and Gilbert returned to Aldwyn's back, and a new illusion was cast, this time of a large raccoon. They hustled around the next bend in the road, and just as Gilbert had promised, there was a small inn before them.

"There's a back door to the kitchen," Gilbert said. "I've gotten pretty chummy with the chef."

Sure enough, the rear entrance was left open a crack, allowing the trio easy access. The kitchen already had a pot hanging above the fire pit, and all that was needed was to ignite the logs and fill up the cauldron.

Skylar let the illusion fade and got to work. Aldwyn pulled the curtains closed, then locked the door to the dining room and the one leading to the outside to make sure no one disturbed them. With the help of a flame fairy, the wood was set ablaze, and Skylar began filling the pot with all forty-three components.

Aldwyn kept half an eye on her progress, but was more concerned with peeking through the curtains.

Wizards and soldiers would run past, shouting and yelling to each other. One even stopped to turn the handle on the kitchen door, but upon finding it locked continued on. Aldwyn spied Urbaugh canvassing the area, too. The response to the messenger arrow had been quick. And no doubt Navid and Marati were also out there searching.

Once every last ingredient was mixed in, a sulfurous odor began to pour out from the cauldron. The liquid turned a shimmering gold.

"I think it's ready," Skylar said.

While the smell was wretched, it certainly seemed as if it might be strong enough to wake the queen from her slumber.

"Gilbert, fill up one of those bottles," the blue jay ordered, pointing to a row of clear containers resting on a nearby shelf.

Gilbert grabbed one and dunked it into the cauldron. When he pulled it out it was filled to the brim with the healing potion. He put the cork top back in, sealing the bottle shut.

"Guys, I think I've got an idea of how we can get into the palace," Aldwyn said.

He pointed a paw out the window to the

queen's memorial, which was now on the move. As the statue was paraded through the streets on the back of the horse cart, passersby ran up to it with more offerings.

"You see those flowers bunched up around the base?" Aldwyn asked. "If we can sneak our way onto that cart, they'll deliver us right to the queen's front door."

"Every eye in Bronzhaven will be staring directly at us," Skylar said.

"What better place to hide," Aldwyn countered, "than somewhere no one would think we'd be stupid enough to be?"

Aldwyn used his mind to unlatch the back door, and the Three exited. They ran through the alley, hugging the wall, hiding in the morning shadows until they reached the street. The horse cart carrying the statue of the queen had already moved down the block. Aldwyn spotted Navid and Marati leading the Nightfall Battalion around the perimeter of the Bubbling Vial and all the neighboring buildings.

Ahead a group of the queens' guard were on the lookout, with swords and wands at the ready.

Some were wearing revealing glasses to ensure that the fugitive familiars couldn't sneak by under the cover of an illusion.

"I'm afraid an illusion won't help us," Skylar said.

Just then, voices could be heard calling out from behind.

"Wait for us! We have something to add to the queen's memorial!"

Aldwyn turned to see that it was a group of mourners carrying an enormous basket of flowers. Hurrying to catch up to the horse cart, they were going to be running right past Aldwyn, Skylar, and Gilbert.

"I think it's time to hitch ourselves a ride," Aldwyn said.

As the trio of mourners rushed by, Aldwyn used a nearby crate to vault himself into the tangle of flowers. Gilbert made a flying leap behind him, and Skylar soared in from above. The Three were nestled in the huge basket, the prickles of leaves and thorns brushing against Aldwyn's fur. Through the flower stalks, it appeared to Aldwyn that the mourners were so eager to make their offering they had failed to notice all the extra weight.

The familiars were bounced and jostled as the mourners raced to meet the horse cart. Aldwyn peered out to see royal guardsmen passing them just feet away, completely unaware that Vastia's most wanted were within their reach. The basket of flowers was added to the back of the memorial, and the horses continued on their procession to the palace.

"Now we just sit back and wait," Aldwyn said.

The statue of Loranella and the memorial moved through the streets of Bronzhaven, crisscrossing so the citizens of Vastia could pay their respects. At first, Aldwyn could see clearly through the flowers, but as more and more gifts were added, his view became obstructed. There was still a sliver of an opening to peek out of. Standing along the side of the road were men, women, and animals holding wooden signs with pictures of Aldwyn, Skylar, and Gilbert painted on them. Xs were drawn through their faces. Devil horns had been added to Aldwyn's head, flames came from Skylar's eyes, and fangs crowded Gilbert's mouth.

"Even after all we've done, they still think we're the bad guys in this," Skylar said.

"Cast off and hated," Gilbert said. "As if we're worse than Paksahara. I just wish they knew the truth."

Aldwyn looked to his two friends.

"I know what it's like to be an outcast," Aldwyn said. "People viewed me as a nobody, nothing but an alley cat. Then I became a familiar, one of the Prophesized Three, a hero of the land. Now I'm even worse off than before. But I know I'm the same cat. And you are the same brilliant blue jay and loyal tree frog you always will be."

Skylar and Gilbert brightened.

The horses were nearing the outer gates to the palace, and the line of guards standing outside cleared for them. They trotted through, stopping in the courtyard.

"Just leave the memorial out here," a guard yelled. "Nothing goes into the queen's chambers until it's been examined for curses, poisons, and hexes."

Aldwyn heard the horses being unharnessed from the cart and led back through the gates out of the palace.

"I think we better make a run for it now," Aldwyn said.

"Gilbert, where's the healing potion?" Skylar asked.

"I thought you had it," the tree frog replied.

Aldwyn searched around. Skylar's feathers began to ruffle. They both looked like they were ready to explode.

"I'm kidding," Gilbert said, pulling the vial from behind some flowers. Skylar didn't seem the least bit amused, and neither did Aldwyn. Gilbert gave a sheepish grin. "Now probably wasn't the best time for a practical joke, was it?"

18

THOMPSON WARDEN

Seeing that the courtyard was empty, save for a guard standing on the far side, Aldwyn, Skylar, and Gilbert emerged from the flowers and pushed their way through the cart full of offerings. They jumped down to the ground and made a beeline for the open doorway leading into the palace.

Once inside, they ran for a back staircase used primarily by the palace servants. While it didn't lead directly to the queen's chamber like the grand staircase would, they were less likely to get caught using this one.

"We're still going to have to get past whoever's outside Loranella's bedroom," Aldwyn said. "But at least we'll make it that far."

They ascended the narrow steps cautiously, peering around each corner to ensure that there were no guards hiding in wait. They reached the top and could see the entrance to the queen's chamber across the hall. Skylar was starting to lift her wing to cast an illusion when Commander Warden stepped out in front of them.

"Don't even bother," he said to the bird. The familiars stopped dead in their tracks. "I expected to see you here. Instructor Weaver told me everything, about how you were going into the Dreamworld to contact Loranella in the hopes of discovering an antidote to her condition. Of course, I was skeptical. Why would the very ones who tried to kill the queen be attempting to save her? But I heard you took quite a few components from the Bubbling Vial not long ago. And left a fire burning in a nearby kitchen." Warden eyed the vial in Gilbert's webbed hand. "That's it, isn't it? The potion you believe will save the queen?"

"You have to trust us," Aldwyn said. "We only want what you want. To bring her back, out of the Wander."

A clatter of iron boots could be heard stomping up the back staircase. Warden ushered the familiars into a neighboring parlor and closed the door behind them. There were piles of unopened gifts on the floor, remnants of Loranella's surprise party only days earlier.

"Give me the vial," Warden ordered Gilbert. "I'll have the healers test it appropriately, and if it's safe, I'll make sure they give it to her. In return, the three of you must turn yourselves in. Until this is settled, you're still enemies of Vastia."

Aldwyn, Skylar, and Gilbert exchanged a look.

"I think we should do it," Skylar said. "Once the queen wakes, we'll be freed."

Gilbert seemed reluctant.

"You promise to keep your word?" the tree frog asked.

"I do," Warden replied.

Aldwyn's attention had wandered over to the presents, all stacked high. He thought back to what a joyous occasion the birthday celebration should have been. And how everything that followed never should have happened in the first place. He could make out the cards glued to the gifts. Even reading them upside down, names like Sorceress Edna and Urbaugh caught his eye. So did Commander Warden's. That one took a moment longer to register, though, as it was signed with his first name, Thompson. Aldwyn stared at it. There was something about the upside-down letters that looked all too familiar: udpjbm uosdwoyt. They were two of the words drawn on the familiars' dungeon cell floor. But they weren't words from a different language. They were letters written upside down. And they spelled "Thompson Warden."

Just like the remwalker had said about Elzzup, sometimes you have to look at things from a different perspective. But what about the other words from the message drawn on the floor? Spuowbip wjots sby. Aldwyn visualized the words in his head. The letters spun around one by one. "Has storm diamonds."

All of it now. Spuowbip wjots sby udpjbm uosdwoyt. Left to right they spelled "Thompson

302

Warden has storm diamonds."

It was a message. Yajmada's armor had gone missing from Turnbuckle Academy. Kalstaff, the Mountain Alchemist, Loranella, and the plaque in the Turn protected the storm diamonds that fit inside of it. And those storm diamonds all appeared to be gone. Now it was clear who was responsible. The man standing right before them now: Commander Warden.

Gilbert was about to hand the healing potion over to Warden. Aldwyn couldn't get the words out fast enough.

"Gilbert, no!" he shouted.

But it was too late. Warden held the vial in his hand. He glared at Aldwyn.

"Why the sudden change of heart?" he asked.

"It's you," Aldwyn said. "You're the one who set us up." Gilbert and Skylar looked at their companion in disbelief. "You made sure Kalstaff's belongings ended up at Turnbuckle Academy so you'd be able to take Yajmada's armor and the storm diamond embedded inside it. You killed the Mountain Alchemist. I'm guessing he hid one of the other diamonds in the book that went

303

missing. You probably got your hands on the plaque at the Turn, too."

"You live up to your reputation, cat," Warden said, impressed. "I'm not sure how you figured it out, though."

Skylar and Gilbert's disbelief quickly turned to shock.

"Not that I didn't count on the three of you living up to your prophecy," Warden continued. "Why do you think I framed you? You're the only ones who can stop me."

"There's just one thing I don't understand," Aldwyn said. "If you've already collected all four storm diamonds, and have the armor, why haven't you used it yet? Loranella says it would be destructive enough to wipe out entire lands."

"The diamond in Queen Loranella's crown," Warden said. "It's a fake. The real one is still out there somewhere."

"Why?" Skylar asked. "Why would you betray the queendom?"

"Because I should be ruling this land," Warden said. "My great-grandfather was wronged. If the original Prophesized Three hadn't stopped him, I would be sitting on the throne of Vastia."

"Great-grandfather?" Gilbert asked.

"His name was Uriel Wyvern," Warden replied. "Of Wyvern and Skull. Perhaps you've heard of him."

Aldwyn shuddered at the revelation.

"But I am not alone in this," Warden said. "There are others, even more powerful, backing me. We will restore balance to this land and the Beyond. Even if it means eliminating all those who stand against us now." He looked down at the healing potion. "Oh, I nearly forgot about this. It's a shame, really. You were so close. But there is one silver lining. At least Loranella won't be around to see the destruction of everything she loves."

Warden raised his arm and threw the vial down. An inch before shattering against the stone floor, Aldwyn telekinetically caught it and pulled it back to his side.

"Guards!" Warden yelled for all to hear. "I've found the traitors!" He kicked open the parlor door and shouted again. "Come quickly!"

Skylar took the vial from Aldwyn and tried to

fly for the queen's chamber with it, but Warden flicked his wrist in her direction.

"*Astula yajmada!*" he incanted.

A crimson spear materialized and shot across the room. Luckily, it only grazed a few of Skylar's feathers, but it was enough to ground her.

Aldwyn focused on the pile of gifts and began mentally chucking them at Warden. The evil commander swatted them away with tiny bursts of wind. Warden whipped his hand around and raised a stone spike from the floor that pierced Aldwyn's fur. Pain shot through his body, but the fact that he was still breathing meant it missed any vital organs.

Gilbert spotted some dirt worms crawling out from the shattered stone. He hopped over and scooped a bunch of them into his hand, then started flinging them at Warden as if he were playing a high-stakes game of sluggots. And he proved quite accurate, even without Aldwyn's help, smacking Warden in the mouth and eyes.

A pair of soldiers raced in from down the hall, swords already drawn and pointed at the familiars. Warden brushed the worms from his face.

"They've brought some kind of poison," he said. "They had plans to kill the queen for good this time."

"He's lying!" Gilbert cried. "He's the one who's responsible for this."

"Arrest them," Warden commanded.

Without wasting a second, Aldwyn used his mind to pull a strand of ribbon from the presents and tied one of the guard's wrists together. The other lunged at him with his blade, but Aldwyn telekinetically parried the attack with the first soldier's sword. They dueled, exchanging blow and counterblow. And though Aldwyn was only fencing with his mind, he overpowered the guard and disarmed him.

Warden had seized the moment to run, exiting the parlor for the upstairs hallway. Aldwyn and Gilbert joined the injured Skylar outside the door, and they could see that more guards were charging in their direction. More concerning was that Navid, Marati, and some of the elite members of the Nightfall Battalion were accompanying them.

"I can't restrain them on my own," Warden called.

"Don't let him get away!" Aldwyn shouted.

Despite Aldwyn's cries, Warden's retreat was successful. He disappeared into the mass of troops heading their way, and none of them had any reason to believe he was anything but an ally.

The queen's chamber was so close. If they could make it through this throng—not defeat them, just pass by them—they could get to Loranella's bedside and slip the vial between her lips.

With their path to the door blocked by the wall of guards and soldiers, Aldwyn, Skylar, and Gilbert had no choice but to come to a stop. Navid and Marati did the same.

"It's over. It ends here," Navid said.

"You're letting Warden escape," Aldwyn said.

"What does he have to do with any of this?" Marati asked.

"Everything," Aldwyn replied. "He set us up. He's not who you think he is."

"His great-grandfather was Uriel Wyvern!" Gilbert croaked.

"Wyvern and Skull had no heirs," Navid said.

"Well, Commander Warden seems to think otherwise," Skylar said.

Marati turned to two of the queens' guards.

"Stop the commander before he leaves," she said. "Tell him we want to ask him a few questions."

The men did not budge.

"We have explicit orders from Commander Warden to stand our ground," one of the guards said.

"You don't take your orders from Commander Warden," Navid said. "You take them from us."

"Not anymore," the guard replied.

Navid and Marati suddenly found themselves alongside Aldwyn, Skylar, and Gilbert, staring at a wall of armored, wand-wielding soldiers.

"I suppose we owe you an apology," Marati said.

"Save it for later," Aldwyn said. "We've brought a potion that will save the queen's life."

"It will be a challenge for even the five of us to get to that door," Navid said. "But we'll certainly give it our best."

"Maybe we don't need to get to the door," Skylar said.

"It's the only way in," Marati replied.

"Not necessarily," Skylar said.

The blue jay reached into her component

satchel and gripped a talonful of moist moss. She threw it up against the outside wall of the queen's chamber and chanted, *"Aquatitus, aquatitus!"*

Suddenly the entire wall turned to water. A tidal wave flooded the hallway, soaking everyone in the standoff up to their ankles and leaving a clear path to the queen's bedroom.

"We'll cover you," Navid shouted.

Aldwyn, Skylar, and Gilbert ran for the queen's bed. Navid and Marati did what they could to fend off Warden's soldiers. A barrage of venom blasts and astral claws took out the first wave of guardsmen.

The familiars came to Loranella's side. She looked peaceful, even though she was slipping ever closer to death. Skylar uncorked the vial and Gilbert brought it to her lips.

A second rush of traitorous soldiers managed to slip past Navid and Marati's attacks. They were coming at the three animals with wands and axes outstretched. Aldwyn looked up and telekinetically tugged the cover folded at the foot of Loranella's bed and draped it over the guards.

"Now, Gilbert!" Aldwyn shouted.

The tree frog poured the healing potion into the queen's mouth. As the last drop went down her throat, the soldiers emerged from beneath the cover. They surrounded the familiars and summoned magical shackles to ensnare them.

"Take them back to the dungeon," one of the guards ordered.

Aldwyn, Skylar, and Gilbert stared at Loranella hopefully. But she wasn't moving.

"Maybe I brewed it wrong," Skylar said.

Navid and Marati were no longer fighting. They, too, were being taken prisoner.

"I'm sorry," Aldwyn said to them.

The soldiers began to lead the animals from the room. It really was over.

"Let them go," a regal voice said, bringing everyone in the room to a standstill.

Aldwyn spun around to see that Queen Loranella had awoken. She was sitting up in her bed, very much alive.

19

WELL OF ASHTHERIL

Less than twenty-four hours had passed since the queen had been saved from the parasitic poison. And despite the palace healers' advice that she take a few days to rest and recuperate, Loranella insisted on wasting no time before returning to public view. Her first appearance would be in the palace courtyard, to resume the birthday celebration so rudely interrupted just a few days earlier.

Hundreds were gathered as before, mingling about beneath colorful streamers and floating paper lanterns. Aldwyn, Skylar, and Gilbert had not only been cleared from their alleged crimes but once again they were celebrated as heroes of the land. They could barely take two steps without being showered with apologies and deep thanks.

Jack, Marianne, and Dalton had been released from their temporary detainment at Turnbuckle Academy and were standing proudly at their animal companions' sides.

"I still think this party was a terrible idea," Skylar said to Dalton, flapping alongside him. "With Warden's whereabouts unknown, there's no telling who's allied with him and might still want the queen dead."

"Loranella is making a clear statement to her enemies," Dalton said. "She refuses to hide. And if there are other traitors among us, they'll be exposed, too."

Marianne and Gilbert trailed just behind the others.

"I thought it might be nice to give the queen a little something from the two of us," Marianne said. "I got her this candle."

"Nuh-uh," Gilbert said. "No more gifts. I'm

not taking any chances."

"Gilbert, trust me, this can't hurt her."

"A card, maybe," Gilbert said, still unconvinced. "But that's it."

Just then, Urbaugh approached.

"Excuse me," he said. "Queen Loranella has requested that the Prophesized Three join her for a moment before she makes her entrance."

Aldwyn, Skylar, and Gilbert parted with their loyals and followed Urbaugh toward an entrance to the palace.

"I want to personally apologize for misjudging the three of you," the hardened warrior said. "I was blinded by what my eyes saw, and not what my heart told me. I assure you, it will never happen again."

"We understand," Skylar said. "And accept your apology."

"Speak for yourself," Gilbert croaked. "I'm still mad. You know what they feed you in those dungeons?"

Urbaugh led them through the open doorway and left them with the queen. She was standing alone in the hallway.

"I'm running out of ways to say thank you." Loranella smiled warmly. "First you saved the queendom. Now you've saved me."

"How could no one know who Warden truly was?" Aldwyn asked. "That he was the great-grandson of Uriel Wyvern?"

"I knew," the queen replied.

The familiars all were taken aback.

"You knew?" Skylar asked. "Then why would you allow him into your inner circle? Make him one of your most trusted advisers?"

"He came to me many years ago as a young man. He said he wanted to fight in my army, but feared I would reject him. I asked him why, and he told me of his lineage. At first I told him that was impossible, that Wyvern had no heirs. Warden said that Wyvern had a secret son, and that he was one of that son's children. I didn't think it fair to punish him for the wrongs that a man he never met had committed. If I could go back now, I would do the same."

"He said the storm diamond embedded in your crown is a fake," Aldwyn told her. "And that once he finds the real one, Yajmada's armor will be ready."

"Yes, he's trying to complete what his great-grandfather was unable to. But there was one thing he didn't count on. The whereabouts of that fourth storm diamond. Even I don't know where it is."

"What do you mean, you don't know?" Gilbert asked.

"It was stolen about eight years ago," Loranella said. "My jewel keeper and his wife raided the palace vault and left with a bounty of treasure. The only item that I truly cared about was that storm diamond. I sent my greatest Beyonders to retrieve it. Jack and Marianne's parents." Aldwyn was taken aback. He couldn't believe that Jack's mom and dad were involved in this mystery as well. "Unfortunately they never returned. Additional parties were sent out in search of them, but they found no sign of them, and no sign of the diamond, either."

"Warden says he's not working alone," Skylar told her.

"I hesitate to ask after all you've done," Loranella said. "But I need the three of you to find that diamond before he does. Otherwise I fear that his revenge will destroy us all."

"There's just one question I still don't have an answer to," Aldwyn said. "While we were imprisoned in the dungeons, a message was drawn on our cell floor. Words were written in the dirt that spelled out, 'Thompson Warden has storm diamonds.' They were upside down and backward. But we don't know who could have sent it."

The queen appeared puzzled.

"I really don't know," she said.

"I've been thinking about it," Skylar said. "If we had only looked at those words right side up, we would have understood the message immediately. Whoever was trying to signal us didn't know exactly where we were standing to receive it. Which makes me think they weren't looking at us when they sent us that warning."

"Gilbert, do you remember what you asked me when you saw those words forming in the dirt?" Aldwyn asked. "You wondered if it was my telekinesis that was doing it. What if it was somebody else's? Maybe another prisoner in the dungeons?"

"That's impossible," the queen said. "Each of

the cells has a counterspell within it that prevents those inside from casting magic. It had to have come from somewhere else in the castle."

"What's directly above the dungeon?" Skylar asked.

"Just rock and stone," Loranella replied. "But there is something below it. Abandoned tunnels. There used to be a well that provided water for the palace, but it dried up long ago."

Aldwyn's heart began to beat faster.

"Did this well have a name?" he asked.

"It did, but I don't recall what it was," the queen said.

"Was it the Well of Ashtheril?" Aldwyn asked.

"Yes. How did you know that?"

"How do we get there?" Aldwyn asked.

"A staircase below the kitchen," Loranella replied.

The words had barely escaped her lips and Aldwyn was running.

"Aldwyn, what is it?" Skylar asked.

"Follow me," he said. "And quick."

Aldwyn couldn't move down the palace halls fast enough. He burst into the kitchen, Skylar and

Gilbert trying to keep up. He took the steps two at time, past the dungeon floor, going deeper. There he found a boarded-up door. With a mighty push of telekinesis, Aldwyn bashed it open and hurried inside. It was a large, cavernous room that smelled of mildew. At its center was a ring of stone with a bottomless hole beneath it. Ancient writing was scrawled all over its walls. Melted candles and cups still wet with cider were left behind. People had been here recently. But no one was here now.

"I still don't understand," Skylar said. "What are we doing down here?"

"Gilbert," Aldwyn said. "Do you remember when I asked you to find Yeardley? I had read the guard's mind, and he indicated that the justiciary had taken her to the Well of Ashtheril. During your locavating at the party in the courtyard, your stone didn't move. We assumed that was because it wasn't working. But it was working. It was working perfectly. The well was right here. Yeardley was here. It was her telekinesis that warned us." He looked up at the ceiling. "Our dungeon cell must have been right above here."

"But my locavating never works," Gilbert argued. "Remember when we tried to find the shortest route to the Mountain Alchemist. The stone went all over the place. It didn't help at all."

"No, Gilbert," Skylar said. "The stone was right then, too. The Mountain Alchemist was already dead. He was in the Tomorrowlife, all around us. The stone was trying to tell us that."

Now Gilbert was stunned.

"She must have known we were in trouble," Aldwyn said.

"She can read minds, just like you, right?" Skylar asked.

It was all starting to make sense. He was spinning around, looking closer at the drawings on the walls. There were images of clouds with a different jewel at the center of each.

"We know that the justiciary was working with the Legion of Mindcasters," Aldwyn said. "They must have been meeting here. And I'm guessing they're the ones Warden was talking about."

Aldwyn had been so close to his sister, without even realizing it. Although he hadn't even met her yet, she had already become an important ally.

A long tunnel exited the well from the other side.

"They must have been using that passageway to sneak in and out," Skylar said.

"We need to find that storm diamond before Warden does," Aldwyn said. "And this time, we're taking our loyals with us."

Aldwyn leaned down and his paw brushed past a tuft of black-and-white cat hair just like his own.

"I'm going to find you, too, Yeardley," he said.

Aldwyn's sister was close and Vastia needed saving. Again.

"Come on," Aldwyn said to Skylar and Gilbert. "Let's go find Jack, Marianne, and Dalton."

"Just once, can't we make it to the end of a party?" Gilbert asked. "At least until after cake?"

But Aldwyn didn't answer him. He was already bounding for the stairs.